Sudden Bloom

Leichelle K

For my sister DuJuana

Some Australian Slang:

Chuck a Sickie- take the day off sick from work when you're perfectly healthy

cods wallup- rubbish

bloke- man, guy

dazzler- beautiful woman

good oil- useful information, a good idea, the truth

horn- phone

just-out-of-school-ankle-biter- kid, dumb person

dogs breakfast- darn it, oh man, oh no.

Sheila- a woman

Sudden Bloom is a work of fiction. Names, characters, places and incidents are the products of the author's imagination or are used fictitiously. Any resemblance to actual events, locales, or persons, living or dead, is entirely coincidental. All referenced materials are the properties of their owners and creators.

Chapter 1

Damn, where's that kid [Back to the Future]

Allain glanced at her watch again, trying to avoid taking a sip of her hot chocolate. The last thing she needed was to jump up in the middle of her "blind date" to go to the bathroom. Why in the world had she agreed to this? Her life was fine. She had gone so long without romance she really didn't think she needed it any longer. Coming and going as she pleased had been great now that her kids were out of the house. She was happy to not have a cluttered house and now her kids were pining for her to get a man, so she could have a cluttered house. Okay that's a bit unfair, not all men were clutter collectors. But her children had been on a rampage of sorts trying to marry her off like the eldest daughter. Those three just couldn't seem to be controlled.

The Three Musketeers. Her three musketeers: Kevin, Shannon and Jake. Ever since she had entered her forties they had declared war on her love life and had stalked her relentlessly. Kevin, her "eldest" had been the main instigator. She had thwarted their efforts ever since they had learned about men, women and dating. If they had a male teacher they would try to have her involved in weekly parent –teacher conferences. If one of their classmates had a single parent, she seemed to be regularly invited to one event or other. She used to hate the start of each school year. She had learned to tolerate their expressions of love but wouldn't have minded artwork, candy and cards every now and then.

Kevin had been the first child she had adopted. He was the son of her best friend, Marisela. She and Mari had been inseparable. Her mother had told her she could never be friends with a Hispanic person. That of course had made her more determined to be friends with the shy little girl in her first grade class. Mari had helped her become fluent in Spanish and she had helped Mari become fluent in English. They had skipped a couple of grades in junior high and had survived high school and college together. She had only been angry with Mari twice in their entire friendship. The first time was when Mari married a boyfriend from college.

They had cried together when Mari's parents died and she had been there for her during her first heart break. Mari had been cleverer than she let on. When her husband left her, she never told him she was pregnant. She had drawn up a will and had even made investments in her unborn child's name. A car accident had changed everything. Allain had nearly had a heart attack when she learned that she had become a mom at the age of twenty. Mari had taken her hand and told her to raise him as her own and be happy. She slipped away to eternal sleep only asking her son be called Kevin. That was the second time she had been angry with Mari.

It was if Mari had given up and was leaving her. They had been so excited about the baby and Allain was caught up in the excitement of being an aunt and making sure her niece or nephew never wanted for anything. She had just finished finalizing her grad school schedule when she received a phone call from the police department. Allain had never been an impulsive person but decisions had had to be made at split second speed and she had almost crashed when the attorney showed up the day she was to take Kevin home.

Even though Mari had left provisions and money was not going to be a problem she would have traded it all to have Mari back. Allain knew that graduate school would be challenge. And she had all of a sudden become a single mother. How in the world was she going to raise a baby, finish school, find a job and live without Mari? She remembered looking down at the small baby thinking, 'great, now they are really going to think I'm the hired help.'

She had called her mother thinking maybe now her mom was ready to give her some advice and be supportive. Unfortunately her mom had called her crazy and told her to give the baby up for adoption and get on with her life. She knew her mom would never understand making and keeping promises. She had hoped that this one event would have finally brought them together. Her mom had always been selfish and would continue to think of only herself until the day she died.

Kevin had brought much joy into her life. She had finished school and wound up taking a job at the university that had turned into a permanent teaching position. In a few short years she'd become a tenured professor.

Each day she'd see her wonderful friend's eyes in his. Friend was not completely accurate, Mari was her sister. Mari had indeed been the only true source of family she had ever known. Her mom had been useless and Allain had all but given up trying to have her mom accept Mari as Mari's parents had accepted her.

Mari parents had been everything she thought parents should be. They had been a little leery of her, thinking maybe she was a homosexual out to corrupt their daughter. Allain proved to be a true and loyal friend and soon Mari's parents had accepted her as one of their daughters. They even ran interference when boys tried to come around and made sure the girls were well taken care of. Allain had felt Mari's loss just as strongly when they passed away.

She made sure to teach Kevin Spanish and made every effort to keep all relatives a part of his life. She had to do some strong persuading to get him to go to college. He said it was too expensive and that he would find another way. In the end he had been thankful that she had made him go. He was a successful video game designer and was making way too much money. So much in fact that he felt he could now butt into her life and tell her what to do. Laughing to herself, she remembered telling him to go home, make love to her lovely daughter in-law and get to work on her grandbabies.

Shannon, her daughter had been her greatest defender, at first. She had spouted every Woman's Power War-cry every time Kevin and Jake had said it was time for her to get married. But lately Shannon had gotten quiet, only half listening, a bit distant. Shannon had been the first and last time she would do something just because her children begged her to. Kevin had wanted a baby brother. She had been teaching long enough at the university that another child would not be a financial hardship but she knew it would be an emotional challenge. She had intended to find a boy, leaning toward a Black child but a news story on kidnapped children, especially little girls had made her seek out getting a girl.

Shannon had been three years old. Allain thought with irony how when she tried to find out about where the little girl had come from the powers that be had basically told her to be happy she had a child and to leave them alone. Under Kevin's care Shannon and blossomed from a quiet, shy, little Asian girl to a vivacious, intelligent woman. She had cried herself silly when Shannon was accepted into medical school. She had started shouting when Shannon became a cardiologist and she talked speaking in tongues when Shannon accepted a position at one of the top hospitals in the country.

Shannon would tell her brothers to leave her alone and had become an expert on woman power. In the past two years, it seemed her advocate had burned out and lost steam. Maybe her work at the hospital was getting overwhelming. She was going to have a talk with her soon.

Jake had come as a complete surprise, her baby.

She remembered when she first brought him home. Shannon and Kevin were still very young and now this baby had appeared in her life. She had almost not adopted him thinking, how could a single woman raise three young children alone? Most people thought he was her biological son since their coloring was very similar. She had thought maybe she would be a foster mother to Jake since he still had relatives but his maternal grandmother had warned her that there was so much turmoil and hate in the family that taking him away and keeping him away was a blessing. One look in his brown eyes had convinced her that this was the right thing to do. It had been those same brown eyes that had convinced her to be here now.

Her date was someone Kevin worked with or knew. She was only half listening. Just what I need an overgrown teenager. Smiling to herself she mentally walked through her appearance, not bad for forty-something. She had decided not to flat iron her hair and wore it with a slight curl at the ends. She had applied a light layer of make-up and made sure that she looked her age. Grinning to herself, she used to hate her high cheek bones. Her mom had said they were gifts from the Native American side of her family. She had just rolled her eyes and considered her smile as one of her ethnic flaws as a Black person.

"I should not have gotten here so early." She tried not to wrinkle her nose. She hated coffee. The smell, the color, everything about it. *"Yuck"* she almost said it aloud. She glanced around the coffee house and noticed a young blond studying in the back. She remembered those days. The main dining area was basically empty for this time of day. Since she wasn't a coffee drinker she didn't want to be in the middle of the madness. If her "date" didn't get here soon she may not be able to take the environment much more.

Continuing her glance around the room she smiled at the couple in the corner and noticed a man entering the café. Oh Lord, here comes Simon Baker. She almost started to giggle when she noticed he was looking at her and heading toward her table. Oh you have got to be kidding me. I am not doing a remake of the movie "Something New." *I am going to kill my children, I'll adopt some grandkids.*

As he continued to approach she noticed he didn't look like Simon Baker at all but was just as cute. His hair was blond but not curly, and his hazel eyes were warm and dreamy. Here stomach did a flip flop and she was sure her heart rate increased a few levels. Okay girl get a grip, he is one of her son's coworkers and she wasn't having any of that. Oh no, he's starting to grin. When had her children moved up to practical jokes? She liked a good joke every now and again but this was downright wrong. What in the world could have possessed her children to set her up for this kind of close encounter? *"I am going to kill Kevin. What was he thinking? I'm going to make Shannon and Jake watch and then I'm going to kill them too."*

She quickly made sure she wasn't frowning and placed a small smile on her face. She adjusted herself in her chair, sitting up a little taller as he made his way to her table. He was tall, slender and lightly tanned. He had on a light olive polo shirt, khaki pants and loafers. Well not exactly making a huge fashion statement but since she was just wearing a sundress with Keds she wasn't exactly setting a trend herself. He was standing next to her and she cast all other thoughts from her mind. With one last mental shake she looked up into his eyes. Okay here we go.

Chapter 2

I'm your Huckleberry. [Tombstone]

Wow! That was the first thing that came to his head as he entered the coffee house. He had expected to see a small, petite Hispanic woman and he was not ready for what he saw. Kevin had said that his mom was beautiful, spoken like a true son, but he had not warned him that she was gorgeous. She was a vision of creamy, heavenly chocolate…wait better stop that line of thinking.

He had quickly scanned the café and noticed there weren't many people about. He had seen the couple off to the side enjoying cinnamon rolls with their coffee and the blond bookworm in the back with her nose in a book. He had afforded them just momentarily glances as he prepared himself for this new adventure he was about to embark on.

David took a deep breath and smiled. He swore this was the first real smile he had had since moving here to the States. He had not thought about his native Australia in weeks. His parents had kept requesting him to return. They had even recruited his sisters Janet and Kathryn to start calling on a regular basis. There were times when he would have boarded the first plane and not looked back but he wasn't ready to face his failures back home just yet.

He laughed as he remembered his last call with Kathryn. She had started saying his nieces and nephews were missing him and would turn to petty crimes if he didn't return. He had laughed so hard he hadn't noticed that tears had dropped from his eyes. The scare tactics they were using were downright dirty. He suspected that someone was going to land in the hospital soon or would develop some sort of illness that would seem dire but would be quickly cured once he returned home.

He had only been living in the States for three years. He had enjoyed working for a photographer back home and decided to go into art design full time. He had enjoyed designing for years until he had met and married his wife. They had had a by the book romance, meeting at one of his mom's many events. They had begun talking after a quite dull presentation, enjoying each other company and he was grateful to talk to someone with a similar sense of humor. She was soon accompanying him to all his many engagements, much to his mother's pleasure. It seemed logical to ask her to marry him. What was he now, a Vulcan?

He had not realized that she had such a high level of insecurity. She hid it well behind her classiness, her comedic demeanor and sometimes lethal tongue. Her infertility had been the last straw in her downward spiral. She began to withdrawal from him and took to going to events without him. He didn't mind at first, he hated all the fanfare. Soon she stopped returning home. He didn't believe she was being unfaithful but he didn't understand why she was turning to everything and possibly everyone but him.

His family had even tried to be supportive. He hadn't shared everything that was going on with his parents but he did tell them that something was wrong. His sisters included her on shopping trips and his mother invited her to all her galas. They had even thought a family cruise together might heal the wound that seemed to gap further and further open. The cruise had let too many hurtful things be said and resulted in an awful experience for the entire family. Every time he had tried to help her, she resisted. She finally told him she didn't love him and that he should just take his paints and go.

For weeks he seemed to despair. There were so many whys and no answers. Had he had his eyes closed so tightly that he couldn't see what was really happening around him? He avoided all the events he usually frequented. He didn't even take part in events where his works were on display. His family had substituted but he knew an artist couldn't survive if he wasn't accessible at least sometimes.

After his divorce he didn't think he could have the same joy at home anymore. His so called friends had said he now had a chance to be wild and really enjoy his celebrity. David knew that just wasn't the type of person he was. Sleeping around and partying never appealed to him and he wasn't going to start now. He was still feeling disillusioned by his ex-wife.

How could she think that he was such an ignorant person to only marry a person based on their fertility? Of course he didn't really know that for sure. She wouldn't talk to him about it. But the divorce papers seemed to indicate that sentiment. They had never talked about children while they dated. He hadn't even thought about it personally. Sure, he might like being a parent at some time in his life, but if it passed him by he wasn't really bothered by that. He just wanted a companion. A woman that got him and he got her. He thought he had found that. He had loved her sense of style and adventurous spirit. She knew how to throw a party and found taking charge an easy thing to do. As he thought back on their relationship, they had not talked about much other than grand parties when he opened his own studio or being invited to the latest hot spots. His mother and sisters had always enjoyed the grand parties they had been invited to. His father was a famous architect and this had brought a lifestyle of great privilege.

He beat himself up for weeks over the failure of his marriage. He wanted what his parents had had. Comfort, friendship and companionship. He believed he had found that. He had been wrong. Very, very wrong. Each time he would go to work he felt terrible. Everything he had designed during the time of his marriage he felt were reflections of his mistakes. Maybe he had spent too much time working or maybe he had just been an idiot. Whatever the problem had been, he needed to leave and start fresh.

His first stop had been New York. He had only stayed there a year realizing he had made a mistake going there. His family was so well known it was like he hadn't left Australia. His flaw had been to try and live the same type of lifestyle. Everywhere he went he seemed to be reminded of all his flaws. What caused even more heartache were all the women that seemed to want to throw themselves at his feet. They would break into his office, his apartment or anywhere they thought he'd be. Once the packages containing underwear started arriving he knew he had to make himself scarce and quick.

He thought he'd try it again but he wasn't quite ready to go back home. He found himself in California. He decided to stay under the radar and do things totally different. He took a job at a video game company designing the boxes and overseeing the artwork as it was transported from overseas. His family would have said he was working well beneath his talent.

The small company had not seemed to recognize his name and was looking for just about anybody to help them as they struggled to get their company rolling. It wasn't his dream job but the small nit group was just the catharsis he needed. He got himself a small studio apartment and started to enjoy the quiet lazy days of California. He had started painting again and had even sold a few pieces to some of the fancier galleries in Los Angeles, Santa Barbara and San Francisco.

David remembered the day he met Kevin at a company picnic. Kevin had the freest laugh he had ever heard. After being paired together for the three leg race, he learned how competitive and persistent the young man was. Kevin had brought his fiancé and had been on cloud nine. He had envied the Hispanic couple as they received well wishes from everyone and spoke excitedly about their future plans. Kevin's fiancé had left some time later but Kevin had stayed on to continue having a good time. He noticed a strong character in the young man and decided he didn't need to envy him, but befriending him would be a better course of action.

He didn't realize his new friend was such a big brother type. Kevin began to invite David over for dinner on a regular basis. David had felt bad about not attending Kevin's wedding so he had accepted the dinner invitation to make up for it. He had enjoyed the camaraderie and soon saw a maturity in the young man that he hoped he would grow up to have.

Not that he was old, but forty-five wasn't so bad. He had taken care of himself so he didn't look his age at all. On numerous occasions he had seen the young ladies giggle and want to dare each other to ask him out. He knew he was old enough to be their father and there was no way in the world he was going out with any little girls.

No little girls in sight today. Now he was sad that he had missed Kevin's wedding. He looked into the sparkling brown eyes of the woman sitting at the table near the back of the café. Her hair was in a curly style and she was wearing a blue sundress. Her smile was infectious and he could tell that she had just shared a private joke with herself.

She looked up at him and he noticed her brow lift momentarily before lowering it and placing a tentative smile on her face. So I wasn't exactly what she was expecting. I guess Kevin didn't mention me at any family get to-gathers. Well here goes nothing.

David approached the table and stuck out his hand, "Hi, I'm David. You must be Allain." He quickly jumped back and dropped her hand as she spat her coffee at him.

Chapter 3

Do you understand the words that are coming out of my mouth? [Rush Hour]

Allain almost fell out of her chair. She had just taken a drink of her hot chocolate when he walked up to her, hand extended and introduced himself. She didn't hear much of what he said. She had gotten hung up on the beautiful Australian accent and had almost choked. She jumped up from her chair to grab some napkins, apologizing profusely as he wiped his arm and hand.

Oh Lord he was gorgeous. Okay so the three musketeers have been granted a stay of execution but they weren't out of the woods yet.

"I am so sorry. I think I tried to take a drink, breath and swallow at the same time. '

She believed he said 'not a problem' but she got tripped up by that accent again. He was speaking again. Come on girl you are a college educated professor that deals with bubble gum students every semester. You've addressed persons with multiple advanced degrees, organized multi-million dollar events for the university. What was wrong with her?

Outside? Oh he wanted to go outside. Breath Allain, you are not out on your first date. Correction, it had been a while maybe she was out on her first date.

"I just feel dreadful about this. Did I get any on you other than you forearm area?" He was looking at her fully and said something about how she just got his arm and no other damage was done. He had taken her by the elbow and was guiding her to the door.

Now he was saying something about not really a coffee drinker but for some reason Kevin thought this would be a nice place to meet as he smiled at her.

The mention of Kevin's name caused some of the fog to lift a bit and she began to understand the words she was hearing. "I think I may have watched one too many movies with my son when he was little. I'm not a coffee drinker either. This was my first hot chocolate at a coffee house."

He laughed deep in his chest. She was feeling a tingle up her spine and butterflies in her stomach at hearing his rich voice. She felt her grin grow as he said he understood and explained how his nieces and nephews believed that they were manipulating him, not realizing he had seen that movie way before they tried anything.

Allain laughed softly. "Why do kids think they are the first to come up with their tricks? Kevin had to give it up very early not realizing he had a movie diva for a mom."

"Movie diva? That's a new one to me not that I know all the American slang." He said with a smile.

They had started walking down the boulevard away from the coffee house. It was a lovely June day not quite eleven in the morning and the boulevard had not gotten crowded yet. The plan was to meet at the coffee house and decide what to do for the day. They crossed the street to the park and he took a seat on one of the benches guiding her still by the elbow to sit next to him. Allain was amazed that she hadn't tripped over her own feet. He was speaking to her, gazing at her intently and she felt like she could float away on a cloud.

Allain began to understand why Kevin wouldn't give her David's phone number. She would have fainted upon hearing his voice. My son! And if I find out the other two were in on this....

Recovering from her initial shock she enjoyed hearing everything he had to say. She could have closed her eyes and listened to him speak all day and night. He asked her about her work and seemed to get a kick out of the fact that she taught math to college students. She tried not to stare into his eyes when she answered his questions. She felt he was looking into her soul and she felt her heart rate begin to speed up again.

What was it about him that had her responding so? Okay it had been a long time since she had spent any time with a man and even longer since she had let intimacy be a part of her life. If she kept looking at his mouth she was sure she was going to start sweating and her mind would take her down a road she wasn't sure she wanted to go down.

She had never been loose with her body, even as a young girl but she didn't mind being appreciated for what she had. She and Mari had enjoyed being sexy "good" girls but had for the most part kept their virginities until college. When she became a faculty member she had almost been embarrassed by the conversations her colleagues would have about booty calls and their latest conquests. There were times she felt sorry for the young people some of her coworkers used for their pleasure. She was especially angry when the targets were students.

But David wasn't a booty call, or at least she wasn't going to let him be. He was so good looking she knew she could easily fall under his spell. *His lips were all over her body and the touch of his skin on hers was electrifying.* Where in the world had that come from? Well at least she knew she was still a human woman that still knew what lust was. They needed to get off this bench. She suggested they take a walk.

They walked across the park to where beach began. They had yet to decide what activities to do on their date. The conversation flowed easily between them and they enjoyed each other's company.

"Walk on the beach?"

"Not in these shoes."

"Well, Movie Diva, is there a movie you'd like to see?" David noticed she was still gripping her coffee cup.

"I have no idea what's playing right now. I just finished entering final grades for my students. Is there something in particular you wanted to see?"

Smooth, throwing the ball back into my court. "There's a new independent film playing that I thought might be interesting," he replied.

"I've always liked going to independent films. I could never convince any of my colleagues to go with me. First let me get rid of this cold chocolate," she said with a grin.

David laughed again, "No don't throw it away. Let's save it as a souvenir of our first date.

Allain looked up at him like he had lost his mind but soon started to laugh too. "Okay, I'll keep it and show my kids what a good sport you are."

"Well my car is over here, if you are ready..." They turned a corner and began to walk toward a public parking lot. He walked up to silver Chevy Camaro and let her in the passenger side.

"Kevin made sure to drop me off and told me I couldn't call him for a pick up." She settled into her seat as waiting for him to close the door.

David tried to make sure he didn't seem too excited as he walked around the car to the driver's side. He would get to spend the entire afternoon with this lovely woman. "Kevin is a bossy one for being so young. I rarely said a word when I was in my twenties."

Okay now they were getting to it, Allain thought. So he's not younger than thirty but we still need to come up the scale a little bit more before she was completely comfortable with this. "Yes, Kevin has always enjoyed his role as big brother a little too much. I'm not sure why he's so opinionated and vocal about it."

She listened with a smile as he talked about being the baby of the family. He explained how his sisters enjoyed being mommy number two and mommy number three to him when he was a boy. She laughed when he said he had become content to not say much, ask few questions and just let them handle everything. He said that even though they were married with their own children they still tried to mommy him.

"That's cute," Allain said with a smile, imaging him surrounded by a host of women telling him what to do. "As an only child I missed out on all the sibling rivalry but I got my fill as the kids were growing up."

Allain shook her head as he explained how many times he wished, or prayed or begged that he could miraculously become an only child. Then he asked her was there something else she wanted to ask of him.

Allain's breathing all but stopped. Had she been that obvious that she wasn't completely comfortable yet? Boy was she out of practice. She's got to start playing poker again. How do you ask a person their age? "Nothing is really bothering me, I was just wondering how to ask you something."

She watched him look in the distance for a moment as he softly told her to ask whatever it is.

He was gazing into her eyes and she knew that no matter what his answer was going to be, she was going to have a good day with this man.

"How old are you?

Chapter 4

Dear God, make me a bird so I can fly far, far away. [Forrest Gump]

David wanted to laugh but realized from the look in her eyes she was very serious. Did he look that young? Or did he look that old? He started to feel subconscious. He knew that Kevin was in his 20s and he had expected Allain to be about 40, though he was sure she'd explain the family tree when she was ready.

"How old do you think I am?" Touché. Let's put the ball back in her court for a while.

"I don't believe I've ever been good at guessing games. I know for sure you're older than my son. Not that you look like senior citizen. You seem to be a person who takes care of himself and that may be why I can't place your exact age."

David smiled to himself. So that was the issue. She didn't want to date a kid. Phew. He felt his heart rate returning to normal.

"I'm forty-five." He said with a full smile. "I do hope that is acceptable." He wanted to say more but he noticed the seriousness of her demeanor and waited for her response. Was that relief he saw in her eyes? Had she been dating younger men and found the experience less than enjoyable? He didn't expect her to start laughing.

What am I today, a clumsy teenager? Allain wished she could take deep breathes to calm her laughing. Tears had started to fall and she was thinking that she must look like a crazy lady. "I am sorry. First I spit on you and now I'm laughing at you. Well, I'm not really laughing at you. I am laughing mostly at myself. I'm sure you think I'm a lunatic." She said with a grimace and placed her hand over her eyes.

David took her hand in his and held her gaze. "David I am completely mortified by my behavior, Allain began before he could say anything. I would not blame you if you wanted to take me home right now." She slid her hand from his and placed it in her lap. She was gazing ahead, seeming reluctant to meet his gaze.

"Allain, was all that reserved-ness because you thought I was too young for you?" He wanted to take her hand again but decided to start the car instead. He busied himself with backing out of the stall in the parking lot. He absently made their way to the freeway as he waited for her response.

"Well the thought had crossed my mind," she began. "Kevin had me agree to be set up on this blind date before he told me it would be with someone from his work. I just assumed everyone at Videxel was under the age of thirty." Allain took a breath and looked out the window. "I know some people don't have a problem with dating people that could be their children's age but I'm not one of them. I feel better spending my time with someone in the same age group as myself and not having to refer them to the internet to know what I'm talking about."

David nodded, "I understand. When I met Kevin he seemed more mature than is biological age. At Videxel there aren't many in my age group there. Though the kids don't really know my age, they've been trying to guess but I've not told anyone but Kevin. There are times that I do feel a bit out of place," he said gazing out in the distance. He wasn't sure if he should continue. He gazed at her trying to gauge her expression.

"Tell that to my colleagues," Allain began. "They seem to seek out the youngest person they can. It's almost a competition to them. Who can have the sexiest, youngest, etc., etc.? Some of the break-ups have been pretty ugly, especially for the ones who are married." Allain shook her head remembering an incident in the office across from hers that had turned violent. Time to change the subject.

"How long have you been living here in the States?" Nice, she was going to start with the easy questions. He nestled into his seat a bit and feeling the V8 engine as he sped up to merge into the freeway traffic.

"I've lived here for three years. One year in New York and two here in California," he waited for the million dollar question of what lead him here to the States in the first place.

"Kevin said you were in charge of the art department." David was a little shocked but regained himself quickly.

"No, I really wouldn't say that I'm in charge. I work with a team that double checks all the computer graphics, but I guess I do have the final say for what goes in the game and what the client will see on the package."

"It would drive me crazy to work with a team of people. I love being able to run my classes the way I want to. I do have to stay within the curriculum that the department sets up but otherwise I am free to teach anyway I want. Of course my raging hormonal colleagues along with raging hormonal college students don't really make me want to work with any of those groups." She turned to look at him and noticed his profile. Oh my, he's a handsome one.

He felt her looking at him. "Bad experience with groups I take it. Of course raging hormones would cause any sensible person to dread them like the plague," he paused to glance her way and saw her still looking at him intently. "I do admit there are times I enjoy working alone but I've got a really good group and we have more success than stress. I guess most of the people at Videxel want to be there so it makes for a better work environment."

"You hit the nail on the head with that," Allain agreed. "Most groups I worked with were comprised of individuals who didn't want to be there or were looking for their next plaything. That made things so unpleasant. Of course each semester I deal with 'groups' of college students, some good, and some bad. So you're not finding yourself lost in a sea of hormones?" Allain asked with a laugh. She always hated the first few weeks of the new semester with the tidal wave of craziness.

David laughed, "You know there are days when I say to myself 'what am I doing around all these kids?' But I love my work. I've always been into art and it's nice to be doing something I enjoy and not have a large stress level. How did you end up teaching at the university? I still don't see you as a math professor." David had parked the car in a public parking lot but was content to just sit and chat.

"It worked out in the most amazing way actually. My best friend and I were finishing up our degrees in math when a professor asked me if I wanted to do some student teaching. Well he fell ill and I took over most of his classes, except calculus. I kept the classes enjoyable and made sure the students had to work hard. I wasn't going to be an easy A for anyone. Anyway, the department liked how students were doing better as they moved up the math track and I enjoyed teaching math. The department made me an offer and I accepted."

She knew she was leaving out a lot of details but she wasn't quite ready to tell the entire story even though they did seem to have some chemistry developing. She had a feeling that if prompted she would tell him everything and that she could trust him with the most private thoughts of her heart.

"I would never have thought you a math geek. As an artist I've always had very little use for math. I like the chaos art allows me and fight against the order that math brings." He enjoyed hearing her laugh.

Allain had removed her seatbelt and swiveled in her seat. She was content to just sit and talk. "I always find it funny that artists seem to have such a hard time with math when unknowingly you use math in almost everything you create."

"No, no don't tell me that. I've enjoyed my delusion. Let me keep my chaos!" He gazed at her and saw the mischievous glint in her eyes. "You know we better get out of this car or I believe you'll be tempted to tell me how art is an extension of math." He bounded out of the driver's side to her side of the car. He had to contain his excitement when she allowed him to help her out of the car.

"I don't know about you but instead of a movie, how but a light lunch and maybe a stroll down the boulevard?" David was determined to just spend time with this lovely woman and didn't want some movie to spoil the so far enjoyable time.

"Are you sure you want to sit at a table with me with food, considering my history with beverages," she said with a laugh. Part of her wanted to protest. She knew that if they kept talking things would turn to a very personal nature and she wasn't sure she was ready. But his smile was so inviting, she couldn't resist. "Okay, you're on but I will not be held responsible for any food fights or wayward beverages."

Taking her by the hand they walked to a nearby café that was redesigned to look like an old malt shop. It was just a little after one in the afternoon so the lunch rush was pretty much gone.

The waitress set them in a booth and began to rattle off the specials. David hardly listened as he stole peaks at the woman sitting across from him. He liked the curls she had in her hair. He knew not to ask question about her hair even though he had the distinct feeling that this was her hair and not additions. She had a small dimple on her right cheek and he was sure if she laughed hard enough the one hidden on her left would show up. She had the creamiest brown skin he had ever seen. He wondered dreamily if I could get her to pose for a portrait of herself.

"And you sir." The waitress was looking at him waiting for something.

"What?" He startled back to the present.

"What would you like to drink?" The waitress looked at him expectantly.

"Oh, well I'll have a Pepsi." He tried not to blush as he glanced at Allain who had buried her nose in the menu. What am I a clumsy teenager? The waitress walked off promising to return soon to take their orders.

"Okay so what were the specials?" he leaned low to ask

"I'm not telling. You were supposed to be paying attention not daydreaming." She laughed.

"What kind of artist would I be if I didn't daydream?" He said with a grin.

"Gonna tell me what you were daydreaming about?" she said with a conspirator glint in her eye.

"Let's just say I've been inspired to create a surprise."

Allain was sure David's eyes were twinkling. What was he planning? It made her think of all the sadistic photographers she had to deal with each time she wanted to get a family portrait done. Well sadistic was the wrong word, but she was sure David would be determined to finish whatever project he set out on. She didn't say anymore when he didn't offer any more on his "idea." She probably didn't want to know anyway since her stomach had started to flutter. She had seen how he had looked at her and he was definitely looking at her like a man looks at a woman.

For the briefest of moments she imagined that they were married and were out for a little lunch together. They would be sitting on the same side of the booth and not across from each other. They'd hold hands and steal kisses as they waited for their food. She shook herself out of her revelry and started to laugh when he ask her, "Who's daydreaming now?"

Lunch had been the most pleasurable experience David had had in a long time. He would continue to regret not making Kevin's wedding ceremony. Look at all I have been missing. His sisters said he needed to get out there again. If this is what they meant, he would have to agree with them. He wished he could read her thoughts. She had a great way of masking what she was thinking; he had never been good at that. Heart on your sleeve David had been in nickname.

He was sure he had caught her daydreaming like he had been doing just moments ago. He wondered if she was having similar dreams as he was. Him holding her in his arms, kissing her till she was breathless or…wait better cool that jet.

"So Allain, if it's not too personal a question…how are you Kevin's mother? Does he look more like his father than you?" David felt sheepish for asking but he was getting more curious as they talked.

Allain finished her bite and wiped her mouth with her napkin. She was glad he finally got around to asking. This was actually a story she didn't mind telling. This was the divining rod that she would gauge his character by.

"I adopted Kevin when he was a newborn. He is the son of my best friend, more like my sister, though we weren't blood relatives. At twenty years old I became a mom. Mari was killed in an auto accident and she had drawn a will, unbeknownst to me, that I was to be the baby's guardian. She and Kevin's biological father had divorced before she had told him about the pregnancy. I entered graduate school without my best friend but as the mother of her son. She named him Kevin and we've been family ever since. I kept up with her family as best I could but when her parents had died years before she died, her family just wasn't as close as it used to be."

David leaned back and marveled at the woman sitting across from him. Not many would take the responsibility for a newborn at any age but for her to do it at a young age and with her own set of goals was more than impressive. "You mentioned you have children. Did you eventually marry and have children?" He instantly regretted the question when he saw a flash of sadness cross her face. Before he could take it back she began to talk.

"I adopted Shannon when Kevin was two years old. He wanted a brother but once I saw Shannon I had to have her. Technically she is my oldest child but only by eight months. But by Kevin's reasoning since I had him first, he is my oldest child. I wasn't going to argue with his logic."

David smiled and reached across the table and took her hand in his. Allain smiled at the gesture and continued talking. "Jake came three years later. I was volunteering at a senior center helping senior citizens learn some computer skills. Well, I met a grand lady, Ms. Lacy who I instantly took to. Her daughter was a drug addict, but amazingly was clean during her pregnancy. Ms. Lacy knew that she couldn't take care of the soon to be born baby and she had legal custody because her daughter knew she was unfit to take care of herself let alone a baby. Ms. Lacy contacted a lawyer had papers drawn up and made me promise to never contact her family once she passed away. I had to take him to church every week and make sure he did well in school. The school thing was easy, but the church thing took some getting used to."

She looked at him and he gently squeezed her hand. "It seemed like a hassle getting up every Sunday, especially since I was finishing up grad school and had three little ones under foot. But it wound up being the most rewarding experience of my life. I found the strength I needed to be a good mother. I was a single mother with three children. We wanted for nothing. Mari had left me money and my job was definitely a blessing. Kevin went into computers, Shannon is a doctor and Jake is a missionary minister."

David loved the look on her face as she described her children. He was even more in awe of this woman before him. To adopt three children and do it all alone. God had definitely kept a special angel for her.

"And before you ask, no I never married. A woman with three children was hardly an enticement. I didn't really mind, I was busy with work and being involved in the kids' lives. Plus it was a great way to keep the riff raff away." She smiled and David saw a sparkle in her eyes. "Of course this meant my children would become crusaders to try to find me a husband, hence here we are today."

David knew he would never tire of her smile. He could imagine Kevin and his siblings trying to set her up with every eligible bachelor while in school. He felt a subtle thud in his heart that she had to journey alone without anyone to take care of her while she was taking care of everyone else. He knew he was in the presence of a rare jewel.

"What about you, any children?" she asked tentatively wanting to avoid the 'ex' question.

"No, my ex-wife and I didn't have any children. To be honest I had never thought about it one way or the other. I figured my sisters were giving my parents grandchildren so I was off the hook so to speak." He looked at Allain and wondered if she had caught the slight sadness in his voice.

"I find great joy in being Uncle David and I spoil my nieces and nephews in the worse ways. It might be a blessing I am not a parent." He looked at their joined hands and let his mind briefly think what it would be like to have a child with her. "My parents are still hopeful, but I'm happy one way or the other. They had hoped that I'd have a few kids by now but my ex-wife was unable to conceive."

David took a breath as he put to words things he hadn't shared with anyone, not even himself if he was honest about it. He almost changed the subject, thinking this was too heavy a subject matter for a first date but his heart told him if she could share about her children, her greatest achievement, he could share his greatest failure.

"For the life of me I still don't even know why we really divorced. We got along and we didn't have any major problems but it seemed like we just weren't the right fit. Once she stopped talking to me and served me divorce papers my only choice was to leave. After the first few months I had to leave Australia. I felt like such a failure. I kept asking myself what did I do wrong, how could I have missed the signs. My parents have the strongest marriage I know, what was I missing that eluded Regia and I. I still don't truly know the answer to that but I have been very happy here in California and I am glad to now be here with you."

After paying for lunch, which wound up lasting three hours they walked along the boulevard, pretending to window shop and just enjoy each other's company. The day soon turned to evening and David tried to think of any reason to extend the date longer.

After plugging her address into the GPS he asked, "So what have you got on your agenda for tomorrow?" David was hoping she would be free so he could see her again.

Allain had gotten accustomed to his accent and was allowing the way he phrased his words wash over her like a gentle breeze. "What am I doing tomorrow?" She leaned back in her seat as he started the car. What did she have going on tomorrow? She knew she had something but for some reason all she could think of was David. She had talked to David and she had immensely enjoyed the conversation. She had lunch with David. She wanted to kiss David. What! Lunch, yes that's right. Her mind starting to work again and she came out of the fantasy. "I have a lunch date with my daughter tomorrow."

David was glad he was driving. He was paying attention to the traffic so he couldn't look at her. He was sure the disappointment would have shown on his face and in his eyes. "Allain I truly enjoyed the day with you and I would love to get together again. Maybe see a movie this time or a play even. I'm not much of a dancer but I have had to glide across a floor a time or two at a gala. Whatever the event I'd love to see you again."

He had said those words with such meaning Allain was sure she had started to blush. "David I had a wonderful time too. And I would love to go out with you again." Why in the world did she sound like some shy fifteen year old.

"Great. I will call you and we can decide. Of course I'll need your phone number."

He pulled up in front of her home and was unsure if he should turn the car off or not. Allain seemed to sense his lack of assurance. She unbuckled her seatbelt and reached for his hand. "Thank you David for a wonderful afternoon and for having a forgiving spirit." She kissed him on the cheek and hopped out of the car. At her front door she turned and waved and then walked inside.

David could not get rid of his grin the entire drive home, which quickly turned to a grimace when he realized he had not gotten her phone number.

Chapter 5

"What's up doc?" [Bugs Bunny]

Allain grinned to herself as she waited for Shannon to arrive. She wasn't sure what time she had gone to bed but she had slept luxuriously and hadn't wanted to get up for Sunday service.

She got up anyway and had some extra praise for what she hoped how God might be marking her steps. She had also hoped the kids would join her at church, especially since between the three they had left thirty messages on her answering machine and cell phone. *Serves them right, the nosey brats, don't come to church don't get any info.*

Of course she had a lunch date with Shannon so she might play it cool to keep the kids guessing. When she had walked into the house after David had dropped her off she had leaned against the door finally taking breathes she had held almost all day.

She was definitely attracted to him but was she really ready or wanting a relationship. She had in so many ways become used to doing things with friends and putting most of her love energy into her children. It had been many years since she had a serious relationship and she was definitely out of practice when it came to men.

She decided to stop her train of thought before she ruined her lovely day. She would think about dating, sex and commitments later, much later.

She turned her thoughts to her daughter. Shannon seemed to be turning back into the shy little girl she had brought home so many years ago. Allain knew something was up, she could feel it. She knew not to push her daughter but couldn't shake the feeling that time was of the essence and she must get her daughter to confide in her.

She looked at the time on her cell phone and noticed that is was fifteen after one. She looked through her messages to see if maybe Shannon had called while she was at church and wasn't going to be able to make it. Nothing, especially since she had called yesterday while she was out with David. I'll wait another few minutes and then I'll call.

The waitress came by and Allain decided to order. No reason to sit here starving. Maybe she should call David to meet her. *Calm down girl; let him make the first move.* Of course it was going to be a challenge since they forget to exchange phone numbers. She had remembered after catching her breath and opened her door to see him drive off down the street. *Boy she was batting a thousand today.*

As she waited for her meal she began to relive the previous day. It has been a wonderful day not counting the slight mishaps. She was sure he wanted to extend things. She had too but her excitement might have caused her to sign her children over to him and follow him where ever he led her.

She could feel her heart skip a beat at just remembering how his eyes locked at her and how attentive he was to everything she said.

She could tell he came from a good home. The way he spoke of his parents let her know she was dealing with a romantic man that had no problem with being known that he was romantic. A man that was confident in himself. At least that was what he seemed. She knew she'd have to get to know him better. There were more questions to ask and of course she had her own answers to give to him as well. She was definitely intrigued about what had actually led to the breakup of his marriage. It seemed he didn't know. Marriage of convenience perhaps? She found it hard to believe that he would do such a thing.

She remembered Mari's marriage. Completely one sided. Mari was basically husband and wife. Allain had never liked Carlos. Most people felt she was just jealous that a man was now monopolizing her friend's time, but Allain was confident there was something more sinister about him than others suspected. For the most part she kept things to herself and tried to be the supportive friend Mari needed. When Mari had ended up in the hospital with a broken arm she made Mari tell her everything.

Carlos had been beating her for almost their entire relationship. Mari didn't know how to get away from him. Of course once Carlos was brought to the table about his horrible behavior he became the model citizen and Mari actually experienced a year of what she thought was wedded bliss. It was not to last. When she landed in the hospital for what would be the last time due to his hands, she called the police and began the process of getting him out of her life. Thankfully they never heard from Carlos again and of course once Allain had learned that Mari was pregnant she understood why she wanted Carlos as far away as possible.

Her thoughts again turned to David. She didn't think he had mistreated his wife, at least not in the manner most wives would leave their husbands for. He definitely didn't seem the insensitive type. Maybe it was just a case of irreconcilable differences. She didn't know anything about marriage or wedded life so any of her opinions were pointless. She was feeling very serious about David and she wanted to make sure she went into this relationship with her eyes open. No hurry, she wasn't in a rush to make a mistake.

She began to feel a little worried as she finished her salad and Shannon still had not arrived. She walked to the lobby of the restaurant and dialed Shannon's number. It rang and then went to voicemail. She walked back to her table hoping Shannon got tied up in a serious surgery and had not had a chance to call.

By the time her meal arrived she was borderline frantic. It was uncharacteristic of her children not to call her, even if they were doing some dirt. She doggy bagged her meal and after paying her bill, she high tailed it out of there. She tried to keep her thoughts positive as she sped home.

As she approached her house she thought she saw Kevin's car parked down the opposite block. What is he doing parking down there and not in front of the house? It must not be Kevin she thought.

She ran into the house checking her messages. She had one. She was hoping it was Shannon.

"Hi Allain. I'm not sure what the rules of dating are and I wanted to get on your schedule before it booked up. I would love to take you out for dinner and a movie this Friday night. My number is 555-475-2012. I look forward to talking to you soon. Have a lovely day."

Well you wanted him to make the first move. Of course how did he get her number? She distinctly remembered not giving it to him so she could call him. Kevin. Rules of dating. She didn't even know what was current when it came to dating. They were grown; they could make their own rules. Hearing his voice made her feel a little better but she needed to make sure her daughter was okay so she could kill her.

She was about to call the hospital when the doorbell rang. She looked through the small window to see Kevin standing there. So he was parked down the street. No doubt waiting to see what was up at the house. My children don't know me very well, she thought shaking her head.

"Well hello there. What brings you out on this beautiful Sunday to your mother's house?" she wouldn't mention that she knew he was staking out her house.

"Hi mom. I was just passing by and I wanted to see how you were since you didn't call me."

"Wait just a minute there young man. I am *your* mother, not the other way around. If I decide to leave town and call you when is convenient for me that's my business. Speaking of calls, have you spoken to your sister today?"

She was looking straight at him and he seemed to shift nervously. Kevin was the worst when it came to keeping secrets. He always got too emotional about it and would have to spill everything.

They had walked to the living room and she sat in her favorite chair. "Kevin, don't make me ask again. Something is going on with Shannon, I know it. She stood me up at lunch and I was just about to call the hospital."

"Mom, I can't tell you. She has to do it" Kevin couldn't quite meet her eyes. He hoped he wasn't saying everything by saying nothing.

"When is she going to clue me in since she's told everyone else?"

"Mom she chickened out at lunch. She was afraid of…mom just wait for her to talk to you please. Plus I'm not here on her behalf; I'm here to see how things went yesterday." Kevin had hoped switching topics would help take his perspiration level down a few notches.

"None of your business, grown folks don't have to answer to you." She wanted to laugh as Kevin's face monitored all his emotions. Maybe I had spoiled him when he was young, Allain contemplated as Kevin seemed to think about his next question. She beat him to it.

"Where is my daughter in-law? I know you told her where you were going and you two are nearly inseparable."

Kevin's phone rang and he answered it. After a few mumbles words he looked at his mom. She didn't realize how vulnerable she is. He had to protect her, even from his siblings.

"That was Lamina. She'll be here with Shannon very soon."

Allain got up from her chair and went into the kitchen. She turned the oven on and began to take various ingredients out of the cabinets. She turned her mind to cooking as she waited for the bombshell her children were about to drop on her. Why the secrets? Why didn't Shannon come to her first? Had she made herself unapproachable in her older years? When had Shannon lost confidence in confiding in her? Had she somehow alienated her daughter and not realized it?

Relax Allain. Let her tell you what's going on and keep your wits about you. She began to pray as she broke the eggs. Guess I'm baking a cake. As she let the mixer combine the ingredients to a smooth compound she began to think about David's message. She had a date for Friday night once she called him back. She almost had his number memorized.

She put the cake pans in the oven just as she heard a car pull up in her drive way. Here we go.

She put two pots of water on the stove to boil and searched for her bag of frozen shrimp. She purposely ignored the opening and closing of the front door and began washing the stalks of broccoli.

She had her back to the entrance to the kitchen. She knew Shannon was standing there. She turned the water off and let the colander remain in the sink. Taking a breath she wiped her hands on her apron and turned slowly. She opened her arms to her daughter.

Shannon didn't say a word as she rushed into her mother's arms and cried.

Chapter 6

"Have you totally lost your mind or are you just plumb crazy?" [Forrest Gump]

He hadn't slept at all Saturday night. His muse had inspired him and he had stayed up until the wee hours of the morning painting and quick sketching ideas as they flowed through him. He didn't believe he had ever felt this alive. Maybe once back when he first discovered art and the passion he had for creating vivid, colorful works.

Allain had been his only thought as he combined colors and patterns and let his heart direct him. He had almost called his family, they'd be up at this hour, but thought better of it. He was getting too excited and he needed to slow down.

When you find a treasure do you wait until next week to dig it up? David knew he was wearing his heart on his sleeve at the moment and he started to panic that maybe it was all one sided and he was imagining things again. He had felt comfortable with Regia but with Allain something was different as if all of his being were involved.

By nine am he was weary and needed to rest. Playing devil's advocate with himself seemed to have zapped his energy. But it was short lived. He picked up the phone and called her. He had memorized her number after answering a call from Kevin. Kevin had said he hadn't been in touch with him mom yet and he wanted to know how the date went. David said he would only tell if he gave him Allain's phone number since he had forgotten to get it from her when he dropped her off. After getting her number David had said that the date went so well that he hoped to have a second date. Kevin had said something about great, she'll be in a good mood and they had ended the conversation. He was hoping she was there. He wanted to hear her voice but her machine answered.

He left a message asking her out again officially and how he was looking forward to talking to her soon. He fell into bed with his clothes on and a smile on his face. His phone rang three times but he never heard it.

By three o'clock he awoke famished and after a quick shave and shower he walked to the local Chinese restaurant for some Nikujaga. He thought about topics he and Allain could talk about on Friday. Food is a good one. Books were a safe area. They could talk politics, though it would be interesting to get her take on international affairs as well.

He knew eventually things would turn to more personal issues. He was operating on borrowed confidence and time. He was comfortable with himself as far as his character and artist sides were concerned. But when it came to dating he felt like a red thumb with a huge garden. He just had never been good at dates. Keeping conversations lively by the umpteenth date were always a challenge. He tried not to think about when the conversation would turn to sex and love. He was feeling more and more unqualified. He knew real love existed. His parents were examples to that fact. Why was it eluding him? Was he so desperate that he was already making Allain the little woman? If he let his imagination take him there, he was sure that he was falling in love with Allain. He wasn't quite ready to fully admit that he most likely was in love with her already. Didn't that seem to be his trouble, not fully being honest with his heart?

David, get a grip, you don't mean that and you know it. It wasn't her race. He'd dated a few women from different ethnic backgrounds, and having an internationally known parent, you get to know the good and bad from all ethnic groups, even your own.

Was he falling in love already? That's it, he really wanted to love this woman and yet he was not ready to tell her about his past or maybe admit some truths the he's finally recognizing about his past. That was the brunt of things, he was ready to tell Allain but actually letting his brain admit it was the obstacle to overcome.

She is not Regia. His mind began to reminisce about of how beautiful Regia had been when they first dated. *She had been your muse too and looked how that turned out.*

David axed that train of thought and looked up to find himself standing at his front door. He didn't realize he had walked back home, he had been so deep in his thoughts about his possibly developing love life. As he ignored those thoughts, he entered his art studio and was in awe as he looked at all he had created the night before.

He had never been so inspired. He was going to keep repeating that phrase to himself all day. He had painted ten different pieces. And though no two looked alike he knew who they represented to him. Most of the canvases weren't pictures of people but mostly of feelings, emotions, tones and hues of life, the images of the heart.

His phone rang knocking him out of his thoughts. He was half hoping it was Allain but he was sure that between the two of them she was the cooler. Of course since she's spit on him she knew that she had a fire inside and he was starting to hope that he'd get the honor of ….. *David you need to answer the phone.*

"YHello?" he began tentatively.

"David, my man. How have things been going? I know it's Sunday and even artists got to rest but I was wondering if you got something new. The gallery is quiet right now and I need something new, fresh, hot, and sexy. If you got it, bring it. I am in need my man!"

David wanted to laugh as he listened to his friend Brannon excitedly chatter into the phone. He and Brannon had grown up together in Melbourne but after college Brannon had taken the first flight to the U.S. and not looked back. Brannon had even lost his accent unless he was terribly distressed.

"Well Bran I might be able to part with a few new items I've been working on. Was there something in particular you were looking for? I can send over some canvases of flowers if you just need some decorations."

"Flowers? Man I need something hot. Fantastic. Out of this world," Brannon all but yelled into the receiver.

David could envision the sweat that was forming on Bran's forehead. "Okay my friend, I guess I've got something in the vault that I can part with. I can meet you tomorrow…"

"Tomorrow! Are you all there? I am in need now. I'll drive over right now…" Brannon whined.

"No Brannon I'll drive over to you. You are too worked up to be behind the wheel of a vehicle." David glanced at his watch, it was almost four. "I'll see you in half an hour."

"Alright David, thirty minutes. I appreciate this my friend."

Ninety minutes later David pulled out of the back parking lot of the gallery that Brannon owned. This was one of many business ventures Brannon had his fingers in. David shook his head as he thought about how Brannon and Regia probably would have been better suited for each other.

Brannon loved high society. The bigger the names, the bigger the stars, the more he coveted to be a part of it. David used to be annoyed when Brannon would invite himself to every function David had to attend. He wasn't bothered that his friend wanted to tag along, he just hated how Brannon would conveniently disappear after making "connections."

He and Brannon had a cool friendship and David was content to keep it that way. Brannon wanted to be a star and David was glad to stay behind the scenes. David had to suppress a laugh when he handed over three of his masterpieces. Brannon had fussed and almost whined over the pieces. Displaying dramatic sorrow at how was he to make any money of these syrupy canvases. David smiled when he passed by the front of the gallery seeing one of his pieces prominently displayed in the main front window.

Chapter 7

She closed the door to the guest room that Shannon was sleeping in. She sat in her favorite chair and waited for her own tears to fall. She actually felt numb.

She had done superbly. She had sat and listened. She didn't offer a quick fix or a solution. She just let Shannon tell her everything. Everything. There were times when she wanted to scream, cuss like a sailor, jump up and down and strangle something.

She had stroked Shannon's hair while the tale came out little by little. Her level headed, smart girl was hurting and there wasn't anything she could do about it.

She absent-mindedly picked up the phone and dialed David. She got his answering machine. She hung up before she could leave a message. *"Well I am not going to sit here and feel sorry for myself."* She grabbed a jacket off the door, her wallet, and keys and headed for her car. She had been driving for an hour when she realized she had no idea where she was going. She parked and decided it might be better if she walked, that way she would not cause a serious accident.

The quaint little downtown boasted of having the most specialty shops in the world. She causally looked in the window and decided people were nuts to pay some of the prices she saw. She paused outside the lingerie shop and contemplated going in. *"For what reason would you need an outfit like that?"* She laughed as she pictured herself with hair parted down the middle with ponytails on either side in big red bows. *"Okay, it's been a long time and maybe I'm feeling the after effects of being in the company of a handsome man."* She shook her head and continued on down the street.

She had gotten to the corner when a picture caught her eye. The canvas was displayed alone with various scarves and silks surrounding it. She had never seen anything so breathtaking. The colors were gentle yet striking. She felt like she could wrap herself in the canvas and stay there forever. The colors added together like a mathematical equation. A single tear slid down her cheek and she blinked a few times to clear her vision. Why was she letting this picture make her so emotional? She was just about to pull out her cell phone when she felt someone looking at her. She knew she had lingered in front of this window too long. She wiped her tears and was about to turn away when she heard her name.

"Allain, what are you doing here?" The question had felt like a gentle breeze.

She looked up and saw David. She didn't even think when she walked over to him and wrapped her arms around his waist. She didn't say anything but put her head on his shoulder and closed her eyes.

She breathed in his scent and let it relax her. She dreamed she belonged to him and that he would take all her troubles away. She was determined not to start crying. She took a few breaths and finally stepped back from him.

"Sorry about that," she began sheepishly. "I've had a crazy, weird day and I guess I just needed a hug. Though how is it that you're here? Are you stalking me?"

David reached for her hand, trying to smooth out the concern furled on his brow. Something was wrong but he didn't want to push. He would readily take her back in his arms if she needed it. "You've been crying."

She looked up at him, thankful that he didn't ask why or try to rush any information out of her. He was rubbing his thumb back and forth on her hand. David led her to an outside café that had tables and chairs arranged intimately to share assorted sweets and desserts. Allain got comfortable as he sat close to her with his arm on the back of her chair. She felt some tension leave her body as she gazed out into the street.

"My day had started very nice. Of course it started with the great day we had yesterday. I woke up this morning, ate my Wheaties and got to church on time. Nothing out of the ordinary. But that was when things changed. I was supposed to meet my daughter for lunch and she was a no show. I get home and Kevin was there. For some reason he was running interference for Shannon. I was trying not to worry or engage my imagination in crazy speculations but I was about to jump out of my skin. Well finally my daughter comes in and she cries in my arms for twenty minutes. I don't say a word I just let her cry."

Allain paused to loosen the grip she had on David's hand. She hadn't realized she was squeezing so hard. Wiping a tear threatening to fall she continued. David put his arm around her shoulders and drew her to him. Taking a breath she continued.

"My Shannon has always been level headed, smart, and quick on her feet. I was thrilled when she got accepted into medical school. She had always been fascinated by the human heart. Every biology or chemistry project was always about the heart. I soon knew more about my heart than I wanted to know."

David watched as she took a sip of her water. He could tell her heart was heavy and it was breaking his that he couldn't do more, say more, anything. He gently massaged her shoulder encouraging her to continue.

"In recent months we hadn't talked as often as we usually do. In the past couple years after Kevin got married we all didn't quite take the time to check in and see how each other was doing. Of course my kids were trying to fix me up on dates, so avoiding them was helpful to my sanity."

"I was getting busy with end of the semester assignments and department meetings. Shannon was starting her residency in cardiology. As long as I wasn't getting a call in the middle of the night I had no reason to think anything was wrong."

"Shannon had been my biggest defender when the boys would try to force me to go out and be social. But recently she had backed off. She'd even started taking the boys side. I found it unusual but not extremely so." She paused while David ordered a slice of cheesecake from the waitress.

"I was looking forward to my lunch date today. I wanted to reconnect, see how things were going and how she liked her new position. I did not expect her to not be there and I was definitely on high alert when my son shows up. I was very suspicious. I started baking a cake and made some gumbo just to keep busy. "

"Shannon said she had met him will she was deciding on where to do her residency. They had been friendly but nothing more. A couple of years ago they ran into each other at a conference and had spent much of the weekend together. They were soon corresponding on a regular basis and soon they began to go out regularly."

David could sense that she was coming to the dark part of her story. He was almost sure that he could finish the story for her. It was like he was hearing his sister Rebecca's life. He gently squeezed her hand to continue.

"It seems my daughter had been seeing this man for a year and a half. She was making plans but it seems he had a different agenda. Of course when she learned he had a wife and family she was crushed. She always thought herself as someone who could see the forest for the trees. But he had fooled her, and as she would soon learn fooled others as well."

"So now my grown doctor daughter is hiding out at my house and is trying to decide what to do. I wanted to be angry with her. One, for not introducing us to him in the first place. Two, for not saying anything to me at all. And thirdly for taking so long to come and talk to me." She had moved out of his embrace and was sitting a little straighter. She was getting her strength back. David marveled at how she seemed to be bouncing back to the woman he had only met yesterday. He wanted to say something to her but wasn't really sure what to say. He knew she wasn't done.

"So looks like I'm getting a new name. Just call me grandma."

Chapter 8

"You can't handle the truth."[A Few Good Men]

He knew it. It was as if Rebecca was living her life through Allain's daughter. Rebecca had been a student teacher and she had fallen in love with her mentor professor. She had kept it all secret and not told anyone. The family had commented on how happy she seemed to be and chalked it up to her just being excited about her new teaching position.

Just as quickly as she had been up she had crashed. All of a sudden she was missing family engagements and seemed too busy to do the usual family events.

He remembered the day his mom had barged into his sister's apartment and taken charge. She had basically locked herself in her sister's apartment and said they would not be leaving it until she got the entire truth.

Rebecca had held out for one day but soon couldn't take it any longer. He hadn't heard the complete details but he was sure his mom engaged some dramatic form of children-aging-her-before-her-time and super tears to get some answers. No one was immune to super tears.

Rebecca had not only given her heart and large sums of money to her mentor professor, she was expecting his child. What hurt Rebecca most was his denial of the affair and the relationship. Rebecca knew her parents were going to be disappointed but she also didn't realize that they were more than willing to be her advocates as well. They moved her back home and told her to take her time about deciding what to do. She kept teaching until the end of the school year and then resigned.

Since she decided not to terminate the pregnancy, their parents tried to not give an opinion on whether or not she should keep the baby. David had never seen his mother so mellow and calm. He remembered a time when the caterer had delivered the wrong menu items and the art gallery staff had displayed all the artwork upside down. Her fury had even made his father keep a distance. They would later learn that it was true you have to watch the quiet ones. When a similar debacle happened at another art gallery that had boasted that they were the best in the business. His mom had not said a word; she had seemed to take it in stride. It wasn't even twenty-four hours before the gallery was defunct and no one would dare showcase any works there.

Once Rebecca decided to keep the child, their mom got the family legal team to draw papers to make sure the father would never be able to stake any claim on the child. Rebecca had never disclosed which family she was a member of.

Rebecca began to receive flowers and gifts. Her former lover would try to call and send letters. Dad would not let anything from him onto the property. Mom destroyed everything he sent. When he realized wooing Rebecca back was not going to work he started his own legal pursuit of the child. Of course this meant admitting to the affair and other activities. It had been a messy, stressful time but in the end the teacher was seen for the jerk he truly was.

Rebecca had given birth to beautiful little girl and had turned all her energies into raising her child alone. He smiled when he recalled the turmoil that erupted when Rebecca met Stanley. Rebecca had resigned herself to me the nun-mother but Stanley with a little family help was meant to be part of the family. Stanley had taken to Rebecca's daughter as if she was his own. Of course now they had four little girls and Rebecca was back to teaching again.

David wanted to tell Allain all this but he knew now was not the time. He had almost run a red light when he came around the front of the gallery after dropping off his works. He had begun to laugh at how quickly Brannon had displayed them when he noticed a familiar looking woman gazing into the gallery. He thought his eyes were playing tricks on him since he had been a little sleep deprived.

No it was no illusion. Allain was there looking at his picture. He had quickly found a place to park and had to keep from running to join her.

He watched her for a moment and she seemed to connect with his painting. He moved closer as he saw a tear rundown her cheek. He wasn't sure what to do. She had not noticed him and was about to turn away.

"Allain, what are you doing here?" He had almost whispered it so as not to scare her.

She had turned to look at him. There was a bit of surprise in her eyes but something else, sadness, relief, hurt. She walked to him and put her arms around his waist and rested her head on his shoulder. He drew her as close as possible, enveloping her in his arms.

He heard her sigh and would have been content to do the same but he knew she was upset about something and now was not the time to fall into fantasyland.

As she loosed her hold on him he took her by the hand and led her to the outdoor café next door to the gallery. He didn't think she really noticed him seating her and his drawing her into his embrace as they faced the street. It seemed natural for her to be in his arms, pouring her heart out to him and his listening to every word.

She spoke slowly at first. He could see the pleasure on her face as she spoke of their time together less than twenty-four hours earlier. How am I going to make it until Friday without seeing this woman every day?

Allain become more animated as she recounted her day and the news her children would pounce on her. His heart hurt as she spoke of her pain, anger and sadness. She felt she was a failure that her children couldn't come to her with their troubles. She didn't say it but her body language was one of defeat. And it was saying it quite loudly.

He would periodically squeeze her hand for support and he absently massaged her shoulder and drew her closer into his embrace. *"She belongs here with me. I want to be there for this woman."*

That realization startled him for a minute. He had never felt like this for Regia and they had gotten along for the most part while dating. But he had never wanted to be her protector. Had he really been so caught up in the idea of love and marriage that he had not really given his heart a chance to really love? He wasn't really ready to answer that question about himself. Mentally shaking himself he turned his full attention back to Allain.

She seemed to take from his strength and continued her tale as if she was a million miles away. He knew what she was doing; he had seen his parents do the same thing with Rebecca. Thankful they weren't fatalists and had chosen to boomerang things to the positive.

He wasn't sure why he had ordered the cheesecake. It seemed to stem more from needing to do something than really hunger or a sweet tooth fix. She seemed to appreciate the pause and relaxed a bit more as she continued with her story.

Cheesecake all but forgotten he continued listening to her and watched her transform in front of his eyes. It seemed as she unloaded her burden her strength returned. She was no longer hunched and her face seemed to have a hint of a smile. Nothing seemed to keep her down long.

She had finished and was gazing into his eyes. He didn't really know what to say. Her gaze was so intent that he drew her to him and kissed her gently on the lips. He wanted to deepen the kiss but knew that this was not what she needed. She responded to him immediately, sighing into his mouth and seeming to melt into him. She pulled away first and rested her head on his shoulder.

Before she could apologize he put his hand to her lips. "You are always apologizing for stuff. There is no need for you to tell me sorry. I'm glad that I was able to be here for you. I wish I could have been here sooner." She smiled at him and continued to enjoy his embrace.

David knew his heart had already taken possession and that there was no way he was going to be able to survive without her in his life. He wished he could step out of his body for the moment and watch himself holding her. *Was this possible? Was he actually in love? Was this what he had been missing the first time around?*

"Allain would you like me to take you home?" He asked quietly. "I know the owner of the gallery and your car would be safe if you wanted to leave it there."

"Thanks David but I better get back home to Shannon. I didn't even tell her I was leaving the house." He watched as her vulnerability rose for a brief moment in her eyes.

He wasn't sure how it happened. But as she started to sit back from their embrace, he had started to reach for his cheesecake. They bumped heads and his dessert slid from his hand to her face and then landed in her lap.

Chapter 9

You can love under the best and worst conditions. [Fever Pitch]

She had absolutely nothing to do. School was out and she had a few months before school starts and she knew what she wanted to teach during the new semester. Once the students started registering she could work on her attendance lists and excel files for assignments and test scores. She was on vacation, no reason to start working early.

The house was too quiet. Shannon had returned to her own apartment, Kevin was conveniently avoiding her and Jake had decided to do some missionary work as he neared graduation from seminary. She turned on the CD player to help wake things up.

She glanced at the lovely bouquet of roses on the table and smiled to herself. David had really out done himself. She laughed at what he called apologizing. After their collision at the café with his cheesecake he had sent her a bouquet of flowers every day. Monday had been Sonora carnations. Tuesday he sent English posies. On Wednesday Peruvian lilies had arrived. On Thursday he had sent fringed tulips. He was trying to make me forget about Sunday. *Boy had that been a day.*

She had a bouquet of flowers in every room of the house now.

After washing her face of all traces of cheesecake he had walked her to her car. He seemed to have developed a permanent blush and couldn't quite meet her eyes. She knew the feeling. At least he didn't spit in her face, right?

He had tailed her home and walked her inside. She had looked in on Shannon who was sound asleep and they had sat and talked. By midnight she had to force him out the door. He had to go to work the next day but he was like a kid in a toy store that couldn't leave. He had taken her in his arms and kissed her gently by soundly. She was finding she liked the feel of him and was believing she could get used to him kissing her more and maybe a bit more deeply. Cool down girl, too much of anything can be bad for you.

He had called her every afternoon after her flower delivery and she had to work hard to not have tears in her voice as she thanked him for his thoughtfulness. She knew he was trying to keep her thoughts positive as she tried to be there for Shannon. Friday had finally come and they were going to have their first official date. He had suggested dinner and a movie. Even with their past history of spilling food on each other he had insisted he take her out in style.

Kevin had finally worked up the nerve to call her on Wednesday. She enjoyed making him sweat about meeting David and she really laid it on thick about not talking to her about Shannon. Kevin had taken some of her bluster when he said he had seen David whistling around his office the past few days. Seems he had a major mood lift.

Allain went into her bedroom to look at the dress she had picked out for the thousandth time. It was a deep navy with a V back and swoop collar. She hadn't worn it since the wedding and was looking forward to dressing up again. She had gone to the beauty shop and had her hair flat ironed and gently curled. She was feeling beautiful and was ready to burst out of her skin with excitement.

She was drawn from her thoughts by the telephone. *That must be my baby* she thought with a grin.

"Heelllo!" she said excitedly in the phone.

"Hi mom you're sounding happy," Came the reply. *Whoa, wrong baby.*

"Hi Shannon. How are you feeling?" She was going to try and tread very lightly. Monday morning Allain had woken early and made a huge breakfast. Shannon had eaten some but had not really been in a talkative mood. Allain made it perfectly clear that whatever Shannon decided or wanted to do she would support her.

"I'm doing pretty good. Work has been keeping me busy and I'm thankful for the distraction." Allain felt her pause, but she remained silent. "I still don't know what I'm going to do. I am going to stay in the residency program. I've worked too hard for this to let some eel take it away from me. I'm glad I didn't transfer hospitals because seeing that eel everyday would have been too hard to bear."

Allain thought it was too bad she hadn't at least worked at the same hospital for a little while. She was feeling like a mischievous adolescent and thought scratching up a Jaguar in the most unusual places would have been fun. Her evil twin was begging to come out and play.

"Mom I am so sorry I didn't come to you first. I guess in so many ways I knew I was doing wrong. I didn't know he was married but maybe there were signs that I just didn't recognize and had I included my family I wouldn't have allowed all of this to befall me."

Allain let her finish and slowly released the breath that she was holding. "Shannon I won't pretend that I wasn't hurt, not by your secretive relationship, but that you didn't come to me when things went wrong. I may not be able to correct every wrong or fix every problem but as you mother I deserve, no I've earned the right to support you as you go through whatever it is you are going through." Allain took a breath to continue, so much for treading lightly, "You will have to consider the cost of every decision even more now. Your life is not your own. If you decide to keep your baby, life as you knew it will change. I know. I was younger than you when I became a mom." Allain paused as she glanced at the clock.

"Remember this sweetheart, I love you and there is nothing you could do to lose my love."

"Thanks mom. I am sorry I didn't come to you first. You have never given us a reason not to confide in you. I let my desires blind me to from doing the right thing. I really thought he loved me. Anyway I'll not shortchange my family ever again."

"I know baby. Rest assured you will not be alone. I know the Lord will work this all out somehow. Not that I don't enjoy our chats but I'm sure you need to rest and I have a date to get ready for."

"Mom for what it's worth I'm glad to see you happy. It's about time you let someone love you and that love doesn't require you wiping their nose."

Allain laughed at her daughter's attempt to be positive. "That's my girl. However, no more meddling from you and your brothers. I expect to start seeing you all every Sunday front and center."

"Yes, ma'am. I love you. I'll call you tomorrow."

"I won't be answering young lady. I do expect to see you Sunday morning if you don't have any surgeries planned and then we can go to lunch afterwards and talk."

"You got it. Have a great time."

"Talk to you later." Allain hung up the phone and shook her head. She didn't know how it was all going to work out but she had a feeling that it was. Now all she had to do was make sure she didn't fall in love too fast and see where this adventure would take her.

Right! She had lost the battle when he first spoke to her. He had endeared himself to her during one of her low moments and he had all but possessed her soul with his attentiveness all week. She was overwhelmed by such tenderness. She was sure he felt it too. He eyes told her every time he looked at her that he loved her.

Love. Wasn't it too soon to be in love? She had thought herself in love once before. Seemed like so long ago. That hadn't turned out well at all.

She had tried to date after adopting Shannon. He had been a biology professor from a sister school and their phone conversations had been pleasant. She had been excited to talk to an educated Black man who had more than the typical topics to talk about. They met face to face at a math and sciences conference and had enjoyed each other company. As the conversation turned to personal topics his true personality shined through. He seemed to have an opinion on everything and especially single mothers and Black people with no education. He seemed to be high on his accomplishments and had no respect for anyone who didn't have at least a Ph.D.

When she told him she had two young children and was contemplating another he had been awestruck. There was no way for him to take back all he had said. But she was glad to be rid of the situation in its entirety. She had children that needed her and that were going to be the focus of her attention from now on. Men were not part of the equation. She had gotten accustomed to her lifestyle. She didn't have to deal with foolishness and male drama.

Well her children were grown. She couldn't use the excuse of having little ones to take care of. She could no long hide behind home responsibilities and work.

And she knew in her heart she was ready for someone to take care of her equally as she would take care of him. She was hoping grandkids would help fill that void but she had no right to ask that of her kids. They had to be who they were supposed to be. And if grandkids were to be in her future then they would come. Shannon and Jake weren't even married yet. Marriage is not a prerequisite for children. I wasn't married when I raised my children, though it would have been nice.

Her thoughts turned to David. Now that was a man. Every time he talked her heart skipped a few beats. She could easily lose herself not only in his eyes but his in arms. Was she ready to start sharing, compromising and working as a team? Was she too set in her ways to allow a man to be a part of her way of life? What about sex? She hadn't had sex or made love in quite a long time. Does it come back to you like riding a bike? I guess she really had turned into a nun-mother. Time to burn the habit.

Of course, David's kisses were making her think it was time for a new denomination. Maybe getting married and having a man in her life wasn't as new math as she thought. Had she spent so much of her time developing her defenses that she hadn't thought about what she'd do once she didn't need them any longer? She had told herself that she didn't want the kids to be hurt by some guy entering their lives only to leave them. Maybe she didn't want to experience hurt either and hiding behind her children had given her a safe guarantee. Most guys didn't want to bother with a woman with three young children. And she had become content to not be bothered.

Though there were nights when having man to snuggle up against or someone to vent to and share the burden would have been nice. Sometimes she hated having to be strict or say no all the time. Her evil twin wanted someone else to throw the blame on from time to time. Plus David had ignited a flame that was starting to burn in places she had sort of forgotten about.

Allain's thoughts turned more fully to David and she wondered about his past while trying to shake down the growing desire she felt. She knew he had been married and didn't have any children but that was about it. David was so distracting that she could hardly think straight. She had not been very articulate that day, she thought with a smile. Plus after spitting on him she didn't think interrogation was the way to go. The conversation would stray into deeper territories and sex.

"Lord I'm going to need your help on this one. If this is what you want for me, move quickly because I don't think I'm going to be able to keep my hands, or anything else for that matter, off him." The kids always hated when she talked to God that way. But she told them if you can't be honest with God, who can you be honest with?

She wasn't too worried about sex right now anyway. David was not the advantage-taking type; he was almost too good to be true. A true gentleman to his bones. I'll have to thank his parents someday.

You're assuming much Ms. Allain thinking you're going to meet his parents. She didn't know many Australians. She had no idea how she'd be received. Here international experience came from the people she met at the university. Most countries seemed receptive to Black people and she knew that education had a lot to do with that. Sure there were still ignorant people around, especially when it came down to money and position and she had a few trying times where she had to make a stand and take care of herself. It seemed the United States of American and parts of Africa couldn't get their acts together. Of course people were people no matter the race, nationality or country. When one looks at the world, none of the countries truly have the right formula for just being human and a part of the human race. *Someday it would be nice if all humans wouldn't be so consumed with the outward and just look at the heart.*

Her thoughts were driving her to distraction. Time to clear my mind of philosophy, race and politics. She decided to run out and get a quick pedicure. That should calm her nerves a little. A nice foot massage should help kill some time before her date.

Tonight she was going to enjoy herself with a handsome man and think of nothing else. No kids, no upcoming school semester, no worries.

Chapter 10

The hardest part of love isn't loving someone, but having the courage to let them love you back. [The Wedding Date]

David had tried to stay focused at work but soon saw that it was a losing battle. Why didn't he do a Chuck a Sickie. Not that being at home would have been any better. He was thankful that Kevin was too bogged down in the new game he was developing to notice. How do you explain to your bloke that you're getting ready to treat his mom like a queen and give her the surprise of her life?

He had finally taking out his sketchpad and started to doodle. He thought about the gift he was bringing when he picked her up. He knew he was being a bit over the top but he just couldn't seem to help himself. She had looked so adoringly at his picture in the gallery he had to make her one. He had used the basic color scheme but had added a few touches to make it unique.

He hadn't decided if or more to the point, when he should tell her he's the artist and painting is what he really does. Of course there were more important things he was going to have to tell her. After tonight, I promise. She's going to have tons of questions for me. The flowers all week had been more to build his courage and maybe soften the blow as he told her about his past. She deserved to have the good oil.

Get a grip David, it's not like you were an ex-convict. But he wanted to know about her too. He knew she had never been married and had dedicated most of her life to teaching and her children. But was there someone else from her past that he would have to contend with? Kevin had been silent about his mom and any past relationships. Kevin's response had been that she knew her past better than he and she should be the one to tell him.

He had almost backed out of all the plans he made for this evening. No he hadn't wanted to back out of the date but he wasn't sure if this evening's festivities would scare her or make her mad. In the two years he had lived in Los Angeles he had never used his name to get a favor or special treatment. Today was going to be different. From the limo ride, to the restaurant reservations, to the red carpet entrance he was pulling out all the stops and was ready to give her an evening to remember.

That's it I'm out of here. He gave some paperwork to his secretary and told his team to have a great weekend. He knew all his coworkers had been watching him since the previous weekend. He had been coming to work smiling and a bit more relaxed. Not that he hadn't been friendly before but he knew he wasn't the most open person either.

Once home he showered and began to pull out his tuxedo. He had one back home but hadn't thought to pack it when he moved to the States. He had called up Brannon and asked him where the places to purchase tuxedos were. Brannon couldn't believe what he was hearing. David had played it down, saying he wanted to be ready for events down the road. Brannon had almost jumped through the phone. He had made David promise to do twenty more canvases since the three he had brought in had sold and the buyers were wanting more. Brannon said he had fifty thousand dollars to give him and that once the other works were sold he'd have even more.

David had just shrugged. He had never had a problem selling his work, showcasing was another thing. Regia had always been the manager of that. But now, he thought with a sigh, he was painting from the heart, truly and deeply. He felt that he actually might not mind being a part of the premier of his work this time around especially if the love of his life was standing by his side.

Love of his life. He had tried to stop imaging Allain with their son at her breast while their daughter played nearby. Shaking himself he shelved that dream for later and finished dressing.

At six o'clock sharp the limousine driver pulled up in front of his building. Taking one more look at himself in the mirror he was ready to pick up Allain. He had thought about giving her more flowers but the portrait he was bringing her he felt would be enough.

The driver had come around to open the door for him and he stepped in with the portrait.

David you've wanted to treat this woman special from the moment you laid eyes on her, he mentally encouraged himself, you have nothing to fear.

It seemed like an eternity as he rode in silence to Allain's home. He was thankful the driver did not try to make idle chitchat as they sped down the highway. As the driver pulled in front of the house David felt like it had taken an eternity mixed with the quickest drive on record. The moment of truth had come and he walked with purpose up her walkway.

She answered the door on his second knock and he almost dropped the picture. She was spectacular; she had taken his breath away again. She wore a navy blue dress that had a swoop neck lined with rhinestones and gently hugged her curves. When she stepped back to let him in he saw the dress had a severe V in the back. The dress came to her knees but flared out and down from the sides to the back. It made her seem like she was floating instead of walking.

The canvas he was carrying brought him back to reality and he distantly heard himself say "You look wonderful. I brought a gift for you." He heard her protest saying that he had given her enough gifts to last until Christmas. Should I open it now or later she had asked. He debated with himself and finally said later. He leaned it up against the wall and held out his arm for her. She grabbed her wrap and clutch bag and wrapped her arm around his. He let go of her briefly as she locked the door and escorted her to the waiting limousine.

"Wow a limo. You've told me absolutely nothing about where we're going and I think I'm too afraid to ask," she said with a twinkle. "Should I double check I have a bib in my purse?"

David just laughed, more to relieve his nervousness than anything else. Once they were seated inside the driver closed the door and they were off.

"David I feel like I'm going to the prom. You look wonderful in your tuxedo." She snuggled next to him and gazed out the window. David was almost dizzy with emotions as his chest puffed out even more thinking about this woman sitting next to him. Her neck was distracting him and he had to concentrate to keep his eyes in the appropriate places, with only quick glances, otherwise he might not be able to stand let alone walk.

The limousine pulled up in front of Deveraux's, the most exclusive restaurant in Los Angeles that boasted a requirement of a month waitlist. The restaurant only caters to the rich and famous. David had eaten here only once before when his parents were here on a layover before returning to Melbourne. It was right before he asked Regia to marry him. He almost wished he had gotten an engagement ring for Allain to give to her tonight. That way this experience would be wiped clear of Regia and only say Allain. But he felt a marriage proposal after the big plans he had for her tonight would be too extreme and definitely moving too fast.

The manager showed them to their table and directed the headwaiter to bring a bottle of champagne. Allain sat with wonder at all the fuss and attention that was paid to them. She knew Kevin made some serious money but David was spending more than her assistant professor salary could reach for. I guess art for games pays just as well as the development of the game.

"Allain order what you like. Don't pay attention to anything else. I mean it. Let me treat you as special as you are." He gazed at her intently and reached for her hand.

"David I have a feeling you've been here before." He didn't answer her but instead lifted her hand to his lips and kissed it. He then began to tell her that although Deveraux's was well known for many of their unique dishes he thought their seafood was the best of anywhere outside of home.

David watched as she read through the menu as if she was working on a word problem. He knew she was trying to pick a meal in the middle of the road. Regia hadn't ever tried to do anything like that. His ex-wife had taken to his money life a fish to water. She enjoyed spending while they were dating and she was content to keep it up after they got married. He had never really thought about it. Regia acted just like his sisters and he hadn't thought any big deal about it.

Now sitting here with Allain he was experiencing something he had never known. Someone who wanted to be considerate of him and not because of who he is. *Of course she doesn't know who you really are, does she?* He shook that thought away for the moment and thought how it was refreshing to be in the company of a woman. Someone who wanted to be considerate while she had a little adventure. His heart swelled even more as he watched her behind his menu.

Once their orders were taken he moved his chair a little closer to hers and took her hand in his. He enjoyed touching her and holding her hand was proving just as pleasurable as his fantasies. "Allain I am so glad that you are here with me." He gazed into her eyes and could have sworn the stars where there.

"I told you that I have been married before. I had thought she was my soul mate, the one to complete me. We seemed to have many things in common and I was content to do my work while she did hers. My parents have been married for almost fifty-four years and I wanted what they have. They made it seem so effortless, maybe as the baby of the family that was just how it seemed. Mom would plan huge openings and extraordinary galas while dad would build just about anything that would take your breath away."

"Regia and I seemed to be like them. She could plan a huge gala as well as my mother and my work was impressing collectors and art dealers alike. But for what we seemed to have on the outside we didn't have the connection we needed on the inside. Well after increased unhappiness, she decided to leave me. I don't know if I had been blind or just didn't want to see but I was shocked, hurt and in denial."

"I couldn't seem to function. She had moved on with her life in a blink of an eye and I was still standing by the side of the road. She had been my muse, at least I thought she had been and everywhere I turned all the work I had done seemed to point to my failure as a husband. I came here to the States to try to find my way." He paused to look at her. She was looking at him with soft eyes and squeezed his hand to continue.

"My first stop had been New York but I was hanging with people who knew me, knew my family and I still wasn't moving forward." He took a sip of champagne and continued, "I moved here to LA. Didn't tell anyone I was coming here, not even my family. Most people thought I had gone back to Melbourne. I wasn't ready to go back home, to the many reminders of what a failure I had been. So I took a job at Videxel and actually started to live."

"I remember the first time I met your son. I had felt a little envious. He seemed to have it altogether. You did a wonderful job. I am actually glad I was jealous of him. It made me want to get to know him, see what the "magic" was. He took me as a friend so readily, without any reservations. I had never had a friend like that. People always wanted to be my friend because of who I am related to or for what they thought I could do for them." He released her hand as the head waiter served their salads and bread basket.

"I wanted what your son has. I thought I had that. I had lived in a by-the-book world and just thought things would happen naturally, not really realizing there were some things I needed to do too if a relationship was going to work. I was content to work and let her play." He paused and looked at his salad. "I am sorry I missed Kevin's wedding. I would have met you sooner and not have spent so much time reliving all my regrets."

David saw such understanding and tenderness in her eyes he almost said forget dinner let's find a Tiffany's right now. "My father is Richard Haydon …" he didn't continue. Her eyes had become saucers. She knew who his father was. Almost the entire world knew who his father was. Haydon Enterprises had built buildings in every major city of the world. He father didn't think any job was beneath him and had enjoyed the challenge of putting masterpieces in the most unique corners of the world.

"I see you know who my father is. Well, I guess there's not much more for me to say let's eat."

Chapter 11

The greatest thing you'll ever learn is just to love and be loved in return [Moulin Rouge]

Allain was wrapped in silk and lounging on a grassy hillside under a large tree. The sun was gently warming her skin and she couldn't understand what happened to her clothes. She sat up and watched a pair of swans swim by. In their wake the water began to gently bubble and part. Slowly David rose from the center of the pool. His skin glistened as the water rolled down his golden body. He was saying something to her but she couldn't make it out. He stepped onto the shore and strode to her. He unwrapped her from the silk and picked her up. He continued to talk to her as he tasted deeply of her lips, crushing her breasts against his chest. She almost whimpered when he stopped the kiss. Somehow they were on top of the tree. He laid her down gently, taking in the sight of her. She smiled back at him, admiring every curve and angle. Why couldn't she understand what he was saying? He was kneeling before her now and she began to reach for him. Yes David my love. He was as light as a feather as he knelt above her and began to taste her skin. He was just beginning to travel down her neck when the phone rang.

"What in the world!" Allain sat up in her bed trying to untangle herself from the madness of sheets and covers. "Hello, hello!" Boy did she sound out of breath.

"Mom? Are you alright?" She heard the voice of her youngest on the line.

"Jake, what's wrong, what's the matter? Is everything alright?" She had to get her composure together.

"I'm fine. Wanted to check in and let you know we all made it to Costa Rica safely and I'll try to check in again if I can get a reliable connection. Are you sure you're okay? Did you forget that I was going to call?" Jake was starting to sound concerned.

"No sweetheart I hadn't forgotten. I just got involved in what I was doing and well anyway I'm glad to hear your voice." She wasn't sure how convincing she sounded.

"I'm glad to hear your voice too. We're going to be doing some construction work in a small village so I'm not sure what all the plans are or how things will work out."

"Don't you worry about it. I'll be praying that all that is supposed to happen will happen at the appointed time." She meant that for herself as well.

She glanced at the clock. Twelve o'clock! Oh my. Of course she had had a late night. A late and wonderful night

She still couldn't believe she had dined at the exclusive Deveraux's. The meal had been heavenly and David had completely stolen her heart when he spoke of his past and his failed marriage. She had momentarily gotten jealous of Regia for having had this man for so many years yet not knowing how to be the woman he deserved. Okay she was being judgmental without knowing the woman or her side of the story. Best not to even think about the woman again.

And then when he said who his father was. Everybody knew who his father was. The Donald Trump of architecture. The entire engineering and half the math department all but worshiped the man. He had even designed the university's science building. Everyone wanted a Haydon.

And I'm dating his son. The phone rang again. "Hello?"

"Mom, Mom, oh my goodness! I saw you on television last night. How in the world did you get in to the premier of the new James Bond movie! Was that Kevin's coworker you were with? Mom you looked absolutely wonderful. I loved that dress!"

Allain tried to keep from laughing as Shannon continued to rattle off questions without letting her answer. This was the most animated Shannon had been since their talk almost a week ago. "Shannon, I promise if you meet me at church tomorrow I'll tell you everything. But for now I've got some things to do and I'll have to talk to you later." She hung up before Shannon started rattling off some more questions.

The phone rang again but she decided to let the machine get it. She needed to get ready for her lunch date with David. Mm mm, David. Lord help her.

She thought back to the romantic dinner they had shared. He had indeed treated her like a queen. He seemed to come alive after sharing about what lead him to the States. She had enjoyed her lobster bisque and steamed vegetables. They had shared a slice of pecan pie, with no accidents. He had introduced her to almost every celebrity in the restaurant. She would have been star struck if she hadn't been so in love. She had finally admitted that fact when she glanced down at her salad. He was bearing his soul to her and she had to yield to her heart.

After dinner the limousine had made its way to the El Capitan Theater. There seemed to be thousands crowded around the roped off section of the theater. She almost fell off her seat when the driver pulled up to the red carpet entrance. Taking a quick look at herself in the mirror she let David help her out of the car. They walked down the red carpet as if they were the stars of the movie. When the usher showed them to their seats she was flabbergasted that he had done all this for her.

She could barely concentrate on the movie. The movie was actually very good, James Bond was in top form and the audience had eaten it up. It had been hilarious seeing all the stars act like rowdy kids at an afternoon matinee.

After the movie they had attended one after party and she got to meet Daniel Craig. But it had all paled in comparison to the attentiveness David had paid to her. No matter whom they talked to or where they went, he only had eyes for her. Cinderella could not have out-shined her last night.

The driver had driven them back to his place and he had given her a tour of his studio apartment. She freely let the tears flow as he showed her his art room and all the canvases he had painted. She had never been so moved. He indeed was an artist. It was amazing how he combined colors and hues. He was as storyteller with a paint brush.

She hugged herself, remembering how he took the long way to her house. She hadn't wanted the evening to end either. He had done more than make her feel special. She had felt loved, cherished and completely adored. They had walked hand in hand to her door still unwilling to let the magical night end. He had kissed the breath out of her. She felt her heart rate increase as she remembered his touch.

Allain glanced at the clock again. *I've got to get ready.* No more daydreams time to go see her reality.

Chapter 12

I saw that going differently in my mind [Hitch]

David had finally unplugged his phone. His eyes had been only for Allain and he could have cared less is every newspaper and television station had been on the red carpet.

He had not been ready for the barrage of phone calls. He knew his parents would be first on the horn. It had been great to tell them he was doing well and actually enjoying his time here in the States. They said he looked like he was having a good time and wanted to know more about the dazzler on his arm.

He had tried to play it down; after all, he'd only known Allain seven days. He also knew he wasn't some just-out-of-school-ankle-biter. "You love her don't you son." His dad had always been to the point.

He sounded like an excited kid taking his first trip across the ocean when he described her. The more questions his parents asked the more protective he felt about her. He had gotten so riled that he didn't realize he had promised to bring her home to meet them before he did anything else. Dogs breakfast, he had really done it this time.

When he had finished talking to his parents his sisters had started in. They had demanded he tell them everything. Then he got a call from Brannon. He didn't recall seeing Brannon at the movie but they had seen him at the after party. There had been a few times when he wanted to deck him when he started bragging and showing off. The peacock. Of course there were a few guys he had wanted to deck last night. He knew his eyes flashed "mine" whenever another man glanced in Allain's direction.

Allain had held her own. She had told him she may not deal with Hollywood snobs but they seemed no different than the ones she had to deal with at the university. Her banter seemed to come effortless. Maybe women just have a better knack at this than men.

He had only been able to bear an hour of all the preening and titivating. In the limo ride back to his townhouse she thanked him for a most wondrous evening. She had never felt so special in all her life. She also thanked him for opening his heart to her and sharing his past with her. She knew it had not been an easy thing to do and she admired his courage for putting so much out there with someone he barely knew.

She spoke more of her sister, Marisela. Though they weren't blood relatives their friendship had bonded them together like real sisters. He almost envied the way she described Mari, as she called her, and the life events they shared. He pulled her closer as she spoke of the car accident that would make her a mother at the age of twenty. He could feel her smile as the limo sped through the Hollywood hills when she recounted one of the kids' attempts at playing matchmaker.

Her voice became really soft as she spoke of how the kids' antics always touched her heart. This beautiful woman also had a beautiful heart. He knew that was one of the things that made her irresistible.

She had at one time been engaged to be married. It had hurt to have someone leave you when you thought you were in love. He had done her a favor leaving when he learned that she would be adopting Mari's son. She had tried to date a few times after adopting Kevin and again after adopting Shannon but she didn't have the luxury of playing games and dealing with drama now that she had children. Once Jake came along she only had time for work and the children. Sure there had been times after the kids were in bed when she wished she had someone to recount the craziness the kids had put her through that day. Someone to snuggle with in the mornings and hide from the kids with. God had proven an excellent companion during her parenting years and she didn't feel like she'd missed out on too much.

When he gave her a tour of his home he beamed with pleasure as she immersed herself in his works. He had kissed her tears and held her as he told her what each canvas meant and why he had painted it. He had been so moved he had to fight the urge to call up the manager of Tiffany's to open the store for them.

Was he really ready to get married again? He hadn't been legally married for five years yet he hadn't been truly married for ten. His heart indeed was moving faster than his brain. She had pinned her hair back with a few black wisps bordering her face. She had taken her shoes off and she seemed to have materialized into a vulnerable flower. He knew that she would have let him make love to her but she deserved even more that what his lust was requesting. She had been a steadfast parent, sacrificing her own comforts and pleasures to raise three children alone. She deserved perfection and he was going to make sure he was the one to provide it all and more.

The drive to her house had come too quickly. He knew she didn't want the night to end as much as he didn't. He had meant to kiss her to thank her for being everything and more but the kiss had taken both their breath away. He knew he couldn't go in and she knew she couldn't invite him in or he wouldn't be going home that night or any other night. They would wait until tomorrow to unwrap the gift he had brought for her.

His heart was so full and free. It was as if all his self-doubt had been eradicated. Shaking off all the cods wallup had been a balm to his soul. She knew everything but that didn't change the love he saw in her eyes. Love. He was looking forward to saying it to her; it was something he wanted to tell her. *Remember your dad asked if you loved her too.* Oh yea, the conversation with his parents.

Now it seemed he had one more thing to tell her. He felt utterly ridiculous. He was forty-five years old yet when his parents made a request he had to honor it. Okay let's back track that, he didn't feel completely ridiculous. He valued what his parents thought and wished he had engaged them on more than one occasion when he was dating Regia. He hoped he would get his parents blessing but he knew that he was going to have Allain in his life no matter what. He was certain that with her he could have the love that his parents had for each other.

He pulled his light blue polo over his head, grinned and headed out to his car. Much different from the penguin suit from last night. They had made a striking pair. Once word got out who he was the cameras had descended out of nowhere. He had received over a thousand hits to his webpage and the picture of he and Allain had made the top ten on some list according to his sisters. Someday, hopefully soon he would wake up every morning to her lovely face. He was hoping that lovely face was doing well despite of all new attention that would be coming their way.

He pulled up in front of her house and almost sprinted to the door. She had opened the door on his first knock. He was struck by how her smile always took his breath away. She was wearing a violet sundress with white sandals. "Good morning handsome. Ready to open my gift and help me hang it?"

"You've been peeking haven't you," he said as he entered the living room. He saw the picture was leaning against the sofa, not in the place he had left it yesterday. He noticed one of the corners of the packaging was opened and the backing was lightly gaped.

"I had to get some idea, so I could know where we would hang your masterpiece." She had said with a smile.

Laughing they began to remove the wrapping and he heard her breath catch as she saw the complete work. He'd been an artist long enough to know when he was hearing real appreciation and not just opening night pleasantries. The smile she gave him was all the thanks he really needed. Of course he didn't mind the kiss she gave in the least.

She had picked a spot opposite her favorite chair. She said she wanted to be able to look up and gaze at it anytime. If he got his wish she'd wake up to more than just his artwork every morning.

They decided to enjoy a leisurely lunch in local mom and pop Mexican restaurant. He couldn't believe how freely he wanted to talk. He had never felt this open before. He knew that his desire to share everything with this woman went deeper than anything than he had ever known.

Am I finally on the brink of what my parents have? I don't want this to end. I can't let this end.

But before he could start the new life he wanted with Allain he needed to make sure he had completely let go the old. He needed to deal with his failures and finally forgive himself. He was never going to be all the man that Allain deserved if he was still wallowing in the misery he made himself endure from his first marriage.

They were cuddled together on the couch in her living room. She had shared various picture albums with him, describing the various scenes and memories of the children. Her children. He let the momentary jealousy pass. He would have to be content with skipping the father position and going straight to grandpa.

"Allain, I love you." He had meant to work his way up to that, not just blurt it out. Well, all the cards were on the table now. "I love everything about you and I want to spend the rest of my life with you. I have wanted to propose to you since the first moment we met. If you will allow me, I'd like to make you're the happiest woman alive."

"Before you answer I want you to know that there is something I need to do first. My parents want me to come home, they are anxious to meet you, but I need to go first. There are some things I need to resolve before I can move forward with you.

He was looking into her eyes and he could see the love she had for him. He could feel the courage welling up inside of him.

"Let's go, come on." He didn't give her a chance to respond. He partially dragged her to the car and put her inside. He knew he shouldn't talk on his cell phone and drive but he needed to make sure the manager would be there. "Hello, this is David Haydon and I am on my way."

When he hung up the phone, she had reached over and grabbed his hand. He knew she wanted to give him her answer. He felt her gaze on him as she spoke.

"David I have been so resistant for so many different reasons to what is happening between us. I've gotten used to using the kids to keep others away. Yet here you are, being there for me during some of my unique situations. We both have been given this opportunity for a reason. I don't want to let it pass us by. Everything seems to be happening at once. My answer is yes."

David knew his emotions were threatening to boil over. He parked in front of the Tiffany's and bounded around the car to her side. He let her out, drawing her close to him in a gentle embrace. Suddenly nothing about what they were about to do felt rushed or uncomfortable. As far as he could tell the rest of the world had faded away and there was only them.

They entered the jewelry store arm in arm and the manager had the staff prepared. He had looked at engagement rings previously but he wanted the pleasure of letting Allain enjoy the special treatment they were about to receive.

They browsed the entire store. He purposely showed her the one he had originally wanted to get her last. She hadn't touched any of the other choices but the last one she reached down and held. He heard her say "beautiful." He took it from her and reached for her left hand. He slid the platinum banded solitaire on her ring finger while looking into her eyes. She reciprocated by placing the matching band on his finger. He was now the happiest man alive.

Chapter 13

Only you, you're the only thing I'll see forever. In my eyes, in my words and in everything I do. [West Side Story]

Allain looked down at her left hand for what was probably the zillionth time. She adjusted the platinum band that her oval 2.5 carat diamond rested on. She knew she needed to finish her students' exams but she couldn't seem to focus.

She knew most of her daydreaming was due to her missing David. When school had first started, it had been a welcome distraction while he was away. She was sure he was spending another fortune calling her every day from Australia. She tried not to think about the small fortune she was currently wearing.

She couldn't seem to find the words after he had proposed. She smiled remembering how he tried to tell her everything before she could give him her answer. He had wanted to make sure she had no doubts or fears about the future, their future. Then when he whisked her away to Tiffany's & Co she had completely lost her voice. The staff had been most accommodating, offering champagne and nibbles while they shopped. She felt underdressed and out of her element. David had been all smiles and full of confidence.

Everything they had looked at had been beautiful. How in the world was she supposed to decide? Fortunately the last set of rings had been breathtaking and she knew this was what she wanted. David had finally come clean that he had picked that out for her the day after they met but had decided he wanted them to pick their rings together.

She glanced at the picture of him on her desk. The following months had been a dream. It had been interesting to see the familiar sights and sounds of Los Angeles through another person's eyes. David had a way of finding beauty everywhere, even the La Brea Tar Pits had been a fascinating experience. She hoped that he was finding the peace he needed to bring beauty back to how he saw himself.

He had returned to his home in order to finally deal with the unfinished portions of his life. She would have never have thought him insecure but he still carried the burdens from his past marriage. They both knew he needed to forgive himself and release his past pain before they could begin their life together. Her love for him had grown even more.

Plus they needed this time apart. It was getting more challenging trying to keep their hands off each other. The night before he was to leave had almost been both their undoing. Surely God would forgive her for this one time, especially since they were getting married anyway. David had proven stronger than she and had actually quoted something from a church service he had attended with her. Allain could only shake her head and smile.

The kids had taken the news well. Kevin of course thought it was all due to him and she knew there would be no living with him. Shannon seemed joyous but understandably was unsure. "Mom, are you sure you aren't moving too fast?" Jake had been glad too, he of course said he couldn't give his blessing until he sat down with her beau and had a chat.

She knew the three musketeers were just trying to look out for her, but she thought their over-protectiveness was just too much. She almost wished she had convinced David to just run off to Las Vegas and be done with it. Patience girl, he'll be all yours in every sense of the word very soon enough.

At work she had become Ms. Popular. She was thankful she didn't have to lie when she declined the many invitations to various events because David was out of the country. She turned her attention back to her exams. No more daydreaming for today, time to get some work done.

Allain outdid herself. She not only finished the exams she got them inputted and decided to complete her plans for the rest of the semester. Wow, how love inspires a person. Of course David's quick visits back to California had helped too. He had showed up on her doorstep on Halloween dressed like pirate and she had almost dropped all the candy. He had stayed for two days before flying off to New York and Paris for gallery engagements. Jake was back home so she had behaved herself. He had surprised her yet again by flying in for Thanksgiving. She had almost cried the entire dinner. He had only stayed the day before flying back to Australia to finish some projects he had going on there. She was secretly hoping he'd show up for Christmas and they would take care of their unfinished business. "Lord help me beat down this flesh of mine!"

She used the rest of the day to straighten her office and begin thinking about which books she wanted to order for next semester. She had been approached about writing her own math book. She was seriously starting to consider the idea. She had always published a small study guide through the school's bookstore but hadn't thought of doing an entire book for her subjects.

David had said she should do it. Mathematical books were some of the worst written books in the world he had claimed. She didn't completely agree with him but many mathematic teachers had exclaimed displeasure at the way some material was presented and sometimes the lack of basic teaching was missing from most manuals.

Finishing up in her office she admired one of David's pieces hanging on the side wall. David was indeed talented. When she had to deal with students begging and pleading for points just looking up at the picture helped her remain calm and hold on to her patience a little longer. She was so looking forward to when he'd be back. *Come on Allain this is your chance to get some things accomplished without distraction, she mentally told herself. Take advantage of them while you can, because you'll be planning a wedding before you know it.*

With one final look around her office she turned off the light and locked the door. She swung by a bookstore and picked up a few bridal magazines then headed home to start her real homework. Once school was out for winter recess she could start making some plans.

Several Weeks Later

Allain entered the main lobby of the hospital where Shannon was completing her residency. Shannon had asked her to be at her ultrasound appointment. This was going to be exciting. She was going to see her first grandchild.

As she walked to the elevators she listened to the sights and sounds of the hospital. Trying to have David's eye while observing everyday situations. She was finding it difficult to find beauty when she saw a small group crying together or an angry man yelling at the medical staff. Maybe she should just stick to the fountains and flowers for now. People sometimes made beauty seem like an unreachable thing.

She exited the elevator and waited outside of the cardiology department. Shannon had seemed to be adjusting to the new changes in her life and was starting to get excited. Allain just hoped that Shannon would finish her residency and not give up all that she had worked so hard for.

"Be with you in a minute mom. I am almost finished drinking my water," Shannon called while exiting a patient's room. Allain looked at her glowing daughter. So much had fallen into place for her and she knew God was looking out for them. Shannon had decided to move into a house not far from the Kevin and his wife, who had graciously volunteered to watch the baby when Shannon went back to the residency program.

Shannon broke Allain out of her thoughts and they boarded the elevator for a few floors down. After checking in at reception Allain found herself wondering what it would be like to be pregnant. To be carrying David's child. What would their child look like? Her coloring with his features? Was it too late? She wasn't really interested in having a baby, ten years ago, maybe but now. Of course that was before David. There were other ways that she and David could express their love outwardly that didn't include childbirth. Her heart began to pick up tempo at the thought of having David's baby within her.

The technician called them in and a new world was opened up to the both of them. Allain found herself tearing up during the entire experience. Shannon had started to tease her that if she didn't stop all that crying she wouldn't allow her in the delivery room. Allain had politely told her that it was her right to be as emotional as she wanted. By the time of Shannon's due date in February, Allain was positive she'd be ready.

After the appointment they decided to have an early dinner together. They exited the elevator to the main floor to head toward the parking lot. They had decided to keep the baby's gender private. They were torn out of their revelry by shrill yelling and screaming.

The same man that had been arguing with the medical staff earlier had now grabbed one of the nurses and was pointing a gun to her head. Security was trying to talk to him and get him to release her but he seemed ready to make his point.

Allain turned to push Shannon back toward to elevators but the security guards had decided to make a move. The gun seemed to explode over and over again. The nurse in the gunman's hold went down first and then he began to do three sixties where he stood, aiming but not aiming. Allain heard Shannon scream and tried to catch her as she fell. People were running every direction as the gunman continued his assault.

All Allain could think about was getting Shannon out of there. They were on the ground by some chairs, a few meters from the elevators. "Shannon we're going to have to try and make it back to the elevators. Can you move?"

"I think I can. When he turns his back we should try and make a run for it." Allain nodded in agreement and turned on her side to watch the gunman reload his weapon. She had no sympathy for the man. Nothing, no matter how bad, was justification of this senseless violence.

They heard the sirens getting louder and knew the police were on their way. Seeing the gunman's distraction Shannon and Allain jumped up and began to run to the elevators. At that same moment the gunman began his barrage of bullets around the lobby. Allain heard a bullet whiz pass her ear. Maybe we should have just stayed down, but the chairs would not have offered any type of protection. "Drop your weapon!" was the last thing she heard before Shannon screamed again, this time in pain and her world faded to black.

Chapter 14

Take love, multiply it by infinity and take it to the depths of forever..and you still have only a glimpse of how I feel for you
[Meet Joe Black]

As soon as David got off the plane, he was ready to go. He knew most of it stemmed from missing Allain and not really wanting to deal with the main reason he had come home in the first place. She

105

had been ready to give herself to him that night. He saw so much desire in her eyes he almost fell to his knees. But something her pastor had said a few weeks ago had reverberated in his mind, "Waiting for the right time to have what you want always will equal more than you could ever imagine it could be." He clung to that, wanting Allain to have the best start to their marriage they could possibly have.

The first two months back had been spent with his parents, sisters and their families. He had missed them, plain and simple but he was missing Allain. It had taken the strength of an elephant multiplied by a humpback whale to keep him from bringing her with him. But this trip was for him to repair his heart and make it whole. Allain deserved all of him and he needed to sweep out the hidden fractures that had plagued him for too long.

His parents had been disappointed to see him arrive alone. He knew leaving Allain behind in the States was the right thing to do. He was here to take care of business so he could move on with his life.

He made all the customary rounds with his family and reconnected with many friends in the art world. He had enjoyed making surprise appearance back in Los Angeles over Halloween and Thanksgiving. It had been a good thing that Jake had been there or they may have had to have a shotgun wedding with all the emotion he and Allain had bottled up over the last few months. With a heavy heart he had decided not to fly back for Christmas. He had promised a friend he'd come speak to some art students and no matter how they had tried to organize it he and Allain couldn't quite find the days where they could be together. She was wrapping up her semester with finals and his friend's art class schedule was just as full. Even though he was back and everyone knew it, he was still putting off dealing with Regia. What finally got him motivated was when he went in to talk to the class of young artists.

The students had listened attentively and seemed eager to ask him questions. It was two of the final questions that finally provided him with the extra jolt of motivation he needed to face and finally remove the burdens of his soul.

The first had been what was different between his work then and his work now? The second had been what advice did he have for a new artist?

He took a moment before answering the first question, thinking about his frame of mind then and now. When he painted previously he was doing what he loved but after getting married he hadn't felt as connected to his work as he once had. His works were well received but he hadn't felt the usual excitement when he would share his work with the world. Now, even though he still had some baggage to get rid of, his artwork was more of an extension of his heart and mind working together and not in separate compartments.

He answered by saying he was now painting how he felt and what he wanted, not out of obligation or because it was expected of him but just plain what he wanted. His early works mainly reflected what others had come to expect from him. Now he was doing what he expected of himself. Of course true love is a major contributor but he'd let them grow up and learn that one for themselves.

The second question he first answered with a question. "Do you want me to tell you an answer based on the industry or do you want my heartfelt advice?" The class seemed to ponder his question for a moment and then said give said for him to give them the heart answer.

"Always follow your heart when it comes to your work. Your manager, representatives and publicist will say this is the trend or this is what someone else is doing. Or even this is what is hot or doing it this way will give you more exposure."

"You'll never be satisfied or happy if you compromise or settle just for the money or the fame. What you do will feel like work or a basic job that you have no joy going to. If you paint or whatever it is that you really want to do, the money and the fame will come. More importantly even though you will be working, working hard, you'll be at peace, you will be happy and you won't care what anyone thinks because you birthed something you loved into being."

David had finally been honest with himself. In many ways his second answer had answered both questions. He had been a good son, always did what was expected of him. His artwork had begun to reflect a type of rut he had allowed himself to get into. He was supposed to date and then get married and have a family. At least that was what was told to him as he got older. He had worked so hard to keep his excitement about his work he had fallen short of putting himself into all he did which resulted in everything he did undertake was not as one hundred percent as it could have been. He was so busy being what was expected he had missed all the signs that he was not giving or getting what he needed.

Had it really all been for appearances sake? Had he not truly loved Regia? Had he been so caught up in the dreamy fairytale of love and marriage that he didn't engage in the reality side of it? David shook his head as he headed for the restaurant. His mother had made reservations for them to have a big fancy dinner in town. It was nice to see that some things never change. His mom still loved large, expensive get-togethers.

He had hoped to beg off so he could return to the house and call Allain early so they could talk longer. He had almost sent for her but she reminded him that Shannon had an appointment in a few days and she wanted to be there. He had felt so jealous of his soon to be grandchild.

His mom had teased him about that too. You're going to be called grandpa and having never been called a dad. The more he thought about it he realized that the situation really didn't bother him. As long as he had Allain he was content. But his mother had planted that thought, "Wouldn't you want the woman you love to share in the miracle of childbirth, binding you in ways that would seem unimaginable?" He decided to toss a question up to them instead. "How would you would you like to have a teenager to raise in your sixties?" All of a sudden the conversation had changed to his work that was displaying in the States. In the end he has said it would be up to Allain.

Plus he didn't want to spend too much time thinking about Allain being pregnant because then he start thinking about how he would get her that way. They had done pretty good resisting that temptation but he knew they were getting wearier and wearier. They wouldn't be able to hold out too much longer expressing how they felt about each other.

He nodded at the headwaiter as he walked to his family's table. The restaurant seemed relatively quiet for a weekday but he was sure once his sisters and their entourage arrived the noise level would increase twenty decibels. As he approached the usual spot he was taken aback that a lone figure sat at the table. He didn't see his parents and the table seemed to be made for two. He knew Regia was waiting and he contemplated leaving and not speaking to his mother for a day or two. Shaking off his mild anger and frustration he sat down across from her. "Good evening."

She seemed to have aged from the last time he saw her. Of course the last time he had saw her was in a court room where there marriage had been thoroughly dissolved. Her eyes seemed haunted and even though she was smiling back at him, he saw that the smile was hostage to her lips and teeth.

"Seems the States are treating you well, just like that dark Sheila you've got on your arms these days."

"Sharp tongue of the Outback as ever Regia. Well it seems my mother felt it important to get us together. Should we begin with some fake friendly conversation or should we just get to the gist of the evening?" David hadn't meant to come out so forcefully but he didn't see the need for pretenses.

"Well I'm not sure how to respond to that. Seems you've got some spunk, something I believe I knew you had, which made me hate you because you wouldn't use it." She held up her hand before he could respond. "I want to apologize for not telling you things sooner. Much of me was happy to just live the high life and do my own thing but after all those dreadful appointments and all the disappointments I just couldn't endure your pity love. I knew you would do the honorable thing but that isn't what I wanted. Unfortunately I still don't know what I want but I hate that I took you down in the process."

David sat and just looked at her. He had not expected this type of conversation from her. Though he felt she took most of the blame, he knew he had some share in their failed marriage. They both had married for convenience and the idea of love not really being in love with each other.

"Regia, I apologize to you as well. I don't understand why you didn't talk to me. I was you husband, better or worse. Who is to say that I was the infertile one? You never gave me a chance to work with you about it. There was so much neither of us talked about and we just made assumptions of each other."

David paused and looked at her, "I think I was so caught up with doing what was expected of me that I didn't think about passion and connecting with you. I guess I wanted to have what my parents had so badly that I failed to realize that we are not my parents and trying to make two people into something they are not would never make anyone happy."

Regia reached across the table for his hand, "Thank you for saying that. I know I wasn't the wife I should have been. From the looks of you I'd say you've found what you were looking for. I see it in your work and in your smile. I should be very jealous of this love of yours. You used to smile like that early in your career. That was one of the things that made us girls swoon, your gorgeous smile." Her eyes had turned serious and she seemed to get lost in thought for a moment. "Anyway I've not just be sitting around being a divorcee, I've opened my own gallery and I hope to finally enjoy the industry on my own merits and not just by who I'm married to or should I say was married to or who I happen to be sleeping with."

"Mom always said you had a talent for putting shows together. I believe you'd be great at it. I always appreciated all the openings you organized. I have always dreaded them, even as a kid. I guess mom should have just hired you to be an events coordinator and not pushed for you to be her daughter in –law."

Regia laughed at that, this time the smile meeting her eyes. "Well if my gallery idea doesn't work I just may have to pay a visit to your mom. I do miss her exuberance."

"I understand why mom liked you. You two were very much alike. Maybe that is what plagued me so much about you. We seemed to have the components to have a successful marriage but that just wasn't enough was it? We both needed to discover ourselves and not be recreations of my parents or at least in mind."

Regia wiped a tear from her eye, "As nice as it sounds, being like your parents, I think I felt it first and I hated to burst you bubble so to speak since you seemed content with our lifestyles. I was going crazy. I do feel bad about my selfish behavior. That was so wrong of me, even though I was battling my depression. We never talked and we missed a lot of opportunities."

David squeezed her hand marveling at the most real conversation he had ever had with is his ex-wife, "I never was much of a talker but that doesn't excuse my thinking things would just fall into place. I thought you didn't want to stay married because we couldn't have children. At least that seemed to be what you wanted me to believe. That's neither here nor there now."

Regia squeezed his hand one last time and released it, "I didn't blame you, and though I was heartbroken I knew we could not keep having that kind of existence year after year. I'm actually getting excited about doing something on my own. I hate that I've wasted these last several years trying to be something I am not. I guess I'm done with my midlife crisis."

David's head came up as a light-bulb went on. "If you didn't think it has pity work, I'd love to provide a few works for your new gallery. As a way of saying thank you. We weren't meant to be married to each other but we did know how to take the art world by storm. Also I believe there is someone you should meet. He owns a gallery in Los Angeles among other places and I know he'd be more than willing to give you some pointers or maybe be a partner in your business venture."

"Oh David that would be wonderful," Regia smiled at him again. They proceeded to have dinner and talked like there were old friends. David made a quick call to Brannon and made introductions. Brannon said he'd be on the next flight out. David had laughed and shook his head. Brannon always had an eye for money makers. He had glanced at his watch numerous times but the conversation he wanted to have with Allain wasn't for his ex's ears or anyone else's for that matter He had such a light-ness to his life he thought he was going to burst with joy.

Everything was working out better than he thought. The skeletons were dealt with, the ghosts were gone and now he was ready to go home to the woman he loved. He looked at the clock as he entered his parents' home and debated whether or not to call Allain. He dialed the number and got the answering machine and her cell phone went straight to voicemail.

Disappointed he went to the studio his parents kept on the second floor. He approached the canvas and just let the work come alive. His heart seemed to soar as he let colors and textures take shape. He was still a little shocked in how the "family dinner" had turned out. Even though he knew his mom meant well he had made it perfectly clear that except for the wedding and a few other

115

technicalities Allain is his wife and he would have no one else. Now that all that burdened his heart regarding his first marriage had been excised from his shoulders he was ready for his new life, his real life. Once he finished these works for Regia he would return to his heart and no more waiting. He'd fly them anywhere she wanted to go but it was time to make her his. "No more waiting my love, you will be mine."

Chapter 15

Death cannot stop true love; it can only delay it for a little while. [The Princess Bride]

Allain couldn't open her eyes. She felt the heaviness of the darkness and it scared her. *David where are you?* Every time she tried to shift her body or turn she seemed hampered in her efforts. Why couldn't she move? And why was it so dark? She felt like she had been asleep too long and needed to get up.

She began to work the muscles in her eyes forcing them open. She noticed to her left lights and beeping machines. What in the world are those doing so close to her head? Looking to her right she saw more machines with plastic bags hanging from them. Who had put all this stuff in her room? Where were her pillows and her small portrait that David had painted for her before he left for Australia? Mm, David, she felt her body want to come alive with the thought of him. She knew she was going to have to marry him soon or she was going to be on her knees asking the Lord for forgiveness for yielding to the temptation of some good butt naked sex.

She had almost yielded to her lust right before he left. She knew he had had second thoughts about bringing her to Australia to meet his family. She had almost laughed as he argued with himself about what to do. She had taken his hand and kissed him. He has stopped pacing and looked at her as if she'd just transported from another dimension. She would have loved to have gone with him but she knew that he needed to work some things out from his past on his own.

They had almost become inseparable and she had dreaded the day he was to leave for his home country. He had kissed her tears with such tenderness she was ready to rip his clothes off and forget about everything. He had showed great restraint and had left. Kevin had taken him to the airport and she had enjoyed his text messages throughout his long flight. His poking fun at the tourists and observations of the airline staff had deflated the tension balloon and she started busying herself with Shannon and baby shopping.

Shannon. *Oh Lord, the gunman had shot us. I know I am not dead, I hurt too much.* With a start she sat straight up in bed. Kevin almost fell out of his chair and Jake had run to her side placing his arm around her. "Mom?"

"Jake, help me lay back slowly. I want you to tell me what's going on. Where's Shannon?"

Kevin found his voice, "Mom let me get your doctor and we can start from the beginning."

"Kevin where is Shannon?" Allain had sat back up and saw how her sons were not meeting her eyes. She began to slide to the side of the bed.

"Mom what are doing?"

She pulled her IV stand closer to her as she moved her legs over the side. One of the first things to go is going to be this catheter Allain promised herself. The nurse came and tried to keep her from getting out of the bed.

"What's your name?" Allain asked in her most patient voice.

"Samantha." The nurse had replied.

"Samantha, I'm getting out of the bed and you can either help me with what I want to know or move out of the way. I will not be angry with you but I need to see my daughter and nothing you say or do is going to prevent that." Allain had stated this with a calm demeanor but her eyes were anything but calm.

Samantha regarded her patient and moved to the other side of the bed. "Ms. Krisson I need to make sure all your lines will not be compromised. Let me move a few things and we'll go together."

Allain relaxed a little and let the nurse move the lines around so she wouldn't be tangled up in all the tubing. Allain had just stood up when the doctor came in.

"Good afternoon Ms. Krisson. I'm Dr. Shelton and I see you're up and about. Let me take a look at you before we go out of the room. Are feeling light headed? Pain?"

"I'm feeling some discomfort but I have a high level of anxiety right now about my daughter Shannon that is drowning out everything else. How about you talk to me as we walk to my daughter's room?"

The doctor guided her out the door and to an elevator at the end of the floor. He continued to assess her and the nurse was ever ready in case of a change in her status. They road two floors down to the ICU. They walked a few steps and the doctor turned at looked at her.

"Ms. Krisson, Dr. Krisson suffered some irreparable damage to her brain and lungs. We operated for as long as we could without endangering the baby. She is currently on life support in an effort to have the pregnancy advance before we take the baby. I am truly sorry." Dr. Shelton put a hand on her shoulder as he opened the door.

Allain was determined to not give herself over to tears as she entered the sterile room. Shannon lay as though she was asleep, her chest rising ever so slightly. Allain tried not to think about the machines controlling her daughter's body. She went and sat on the bed, taking Shannon's hand in hers. She felt Jake and Kevin behind her as she looked at her beautiful daughter. She placed her other hand on Shannon's stomach.

"Doctor how long do we have to keep her like this?" Allain didn't recognize her own voice but she knew the question had come from her lips.

"We'd like to get the pregnancy as close to thirty-six weeks as possible." Allain just nodded and stood up. "I'd like to be moved down here. I don't care what you have to do to make it happen doctor but this is now my room too."

Allain sat in the closest chair and looked at her sons. "I need someone to tell me everything. I remember the gunman yelling and people trying to tackle him. Shannon and I were trying to move to an area out of harm's way but I guess we didn't move fast enough. I remember being hit and then I heard Shannon scream. I lost consciousness after that."

Dr. Shelton pulled a stool over and faced her. "You were shot on the left side and left arm. You hit your head on one of the planter vases which caused a serious concussion. You had lost a lot of blood by the time we got to you. Once we got you stable we left you in ICU for a few days and then we just waited for you to wake up. You were in a coma-like state for three days. Dr. Krisson was hit at the base of her skull. We believe she died instantly and if the gunman hadn't been apprehended shortly after you both were shot, we would have lost the baby too."

Allain felt herself go numb as the doctor finished explaining all that had happened and what finally transpired with the gunman. He had killed 30 people and injured 12 others seriously. He would have turned the gun on himself if a Good Samaritan hadn't stopped him.

"Ms. Krisson I'll personally see to you having a bed brought in here but I would like to go back to your previous room to finish your assessment and make sure you are progressing. Will you do that for me?"

Allain only nodded and stood so they could go back upstairs. She looked at Kevin and he came and placed his arms around her. She thought she would cry but no tears came. She then hugged Jake and saw that his eyes were moist and he was on the brink of letting loose. She let him go and started toward the elevator.

They road back up to her room's floor in silence and she proceeded to let Nurse Samantha and Dr. Shelton assess her vitals and wounds. Two hours later her IV was locked off, her catheter was removed, her tube feeding was discontinued and she was ready to move downstairs to Shannon's room.

After her personal effects were returned to her she began to issue instructions to Kevin and Jake. "You two go home, wash up, eat and get some sleep. I'm here now and since my wounds weren't too serious, other than a hit on the head, I can sit here for a while."

Kevin and Jake started to protest but one look from her told them she would call hospital security if they so much as came back before a complete twenty-four hours had passed.

When they arrived back downstairs to Shannon's room, she saw her bed had been set up and an extra chair was off to the side. After speaking with the nurse and volunteering her time to help take care of Shannon and the baby she sat down.

"One more request boys before you leave. Give me a phone, I need to call David."

Chapter 16

My heart is, and always will be, yours. [Sense and Sensibility]

It had been four days. Where in the world was she? He hadn't been able to reach Kevin either which caused him to worry. He had finished a few canvases for Regia and had dropped them off earlier that morning. Brannon barely let him get the canvases unloaded before he was making calls and setting prices. He knew he was free to leave the planet once Brannon and Regia began discussing their new business venture. Brannon had balked at each of Regia's ideas and she had countered with dismay at each of his suggestions.

He had left the gallery laughing, thinking he should have introduced them sooner. He had been so eager to leave he had almost driven to the airport. Then he had decided to buy Allain a ticket instead. He'd bring her out to meet his family and they could still be back in time before Shannon gave birth. She hadn't called for him at the house and there had been no messages on his cell phone.

By the second day he could care less what he looked like, he was beginning to really worry. They had never gone this long without talking even when she had papers to grade and exams to write.

When his phone did ring he had almost cried from hearing her voice on the other end. He was just about to ask her what she had been up to when the sound of her voice caused his ears to perk up. He has stopped breathing as she told him about the gunman and how she and Shannon had been shot. He had raced upstairs to start throwing his things in a suitcase as she talked about her injuries and how she was doing now that she was awake and able to get out of bed. His heart hit the floor as he heard her describe Shannon's injuries and the status of the pregnancy. He wasn't one for science fiction but he would have kissed Scotty to beam him to her at that moment.

He called downstairs for his father and continued to finish packing. He was in the air within the hour. Fourteen hours later a car was waiting for him at the airport and he was rushed to the hospital. He walked right into the room and took Allain in his arms. He kissed her repeatedly to keep reminding himself that she was here with him and he was determined to keep her safe from now on.

They talked in subdued voices and he let her weep until all her tears were gone. He couldn't believe the high level of resolve she had. She was holding it together for her family. Now he was ready to uphold her and be her strength.

Fourteen weeks later

Allain had requested David to be at the delivery of the baby. She didn't have to ask him but she wanted to make sure he would be prepared for the procedure. She hadn't left the hospital since waking up but he had finally convinced her to go home and get some rest and a change of clothing. While she slept he had gone through the Shannon's room and looked at all the baby items. His mother had gone crazy after he had called home and told them what was going on. He had promised when Allain was ready he would bring her home to Australia.

He had installed the infant car seat the day before and picked up the baby bag to take with them back to the hospital. He looked in on Allain as she slept. She looked so vulnerable and small. She had lost a great deal of weight and her usual shine had not returned to her eyes. He had to make jokes to get her to eat and had to use his puppy dog look just to get her motivated.

Her church family had been very supportive but inwardly he was starting to worry. She has single handedly made all the funeral and burial arrangements. As the day neared for the baby to be born she had begun to redecorate the baby's room and pack up Shannon's belongings.

He had offered to assist her and though she didn't tell him, he now knew that she was working through some serious heartache. All he could do was be there. He felt so helpless wanting to do something to ease her pain. When she was ready to talk he would make sure he was ready to listen.

She had asked him to make love to her. They had just finished cleaning up the kitchen and were settling in to watch some television. They were snuggled up on the couch and she was resting her head on his shoulder. He had been rubbing his thumb across her hand and he heard her sigh. She pulled his hand to her lips and kissed each of his fingers. When she was done she put his hand on her breast. He had been so shocked he had forgotten to breath. He looked in her eyes and he saw such a forlornness that he almost gave in to her request. He removed his hand from her breast and touched her chin.

"Allain, this isn't what you want. Baby, I know you're hurting but this isn't going to fix it and as much as I would love to make love to you, you are not really here. I want to make love with *you*. You're back at the hospital and when we come together we should both be together. Just let me hold you."

Her next statement had almost undone his resolve, "David I need to feel you, to hold you. I think I'm drowning and I don't know what else to do." Her voice had been so soft he wasn't sure he had heard her but the look in her eyes told him she was serious.

David was tempted to rip her clothes from her body and love all the hurt away but he knew he couldn't do it. When they made love he wanted to see the passion and fire in her eyes, not pain and heartache. He kissed her and stroked her back. He continued to rub her back and kiss her gently until she drifted to sleep. He carried her to bedroom and placed her in the bed. He removed her shoes and then his own and climbed in next to her. He pulled her close and she melted into his body. He soon drifted to sleep, praying that her heartache would be eased sooner than later. It was one thing to be in pain, it was another story to suffer.

He woke her up two hours before delivery and she gazed up at him in such a way he thought God should give him something extra special for having to endure such a test. He had leaned down to kiss her and she had become so soft in his arms he was ready to stay there forever. She kissed him back with such abandon he knew she was offering herself to him again.

"Allain, baby we've got to get ready. It's time to go get our grandbaby." He watched the war she raged with herself in her eyes. He knew she'd be angry if he let this happen. His heart ached for her but he knew this was not the right time and place for the level of intimacy he wanted to give her when they made love.

Raising from the bed he gently pulled her with him. "I've got the baby bag in the car and I wasn't sure what type of bottles you wanted to use so I packed a little of everything." He walked into the living room still talking hoping to jar her back into the present and give her a little space.

He heard her rise from the bed and walk into her bathroom. *That's my girl.* He went into the kitchen and started making sandwiches. He had learned that he actually enjoyed cooking and it had seemed like a type of therapy as he helped Allain with her healing process.

He felt her eyes on him as he turned to bring the sandwiches to the table. He put the plate down and opened his arms to her. She ran into his arms and he held her, intermittently smoothing her hair and whispering his love for her in her ear. He told her not to apologize, there was no need.

They ate their sandwiches in silence while holding hands. She seemed to have a little more life in her and even smiled. They held hands on the way to the hospital and he didn't let her go when they got to the delivery room.

A short time later the nurse brought a small baby girl over to them. Allain handed the baby to him and went over to Shannon's body. He watched as she stroked Shannon's hair and described her daughter to her. She let the tears flow as she promised to raise her and cherish her just as she had done her and her brothers. After a few more moments she returned to sit next to him and he handed the baby back to her. He let tears flow freely as she held their grandbaby and cried over her. The medical staff ushered them into a regular room and they completed all the paperwork. She handed the baby to Kevin and Lamina and went about completing the paperwork to release Shannon's body to the mortuary. David felt helpless as Allain completed form after form, almost mechanically.

They spent the night in the hospital with the newest member of the family. The baby seemed to be doing fine and the medical staff was pleased with her progress. Because they had made it to Shannon's due date the doctors didn't see any reason for the baby to stay any longer in the hospital. Allain and David had done an excellent job of caring for Shannon's body while the pregnancy progressed.

After picking up some take out Chinese food they all came back to the house with the newest member of their family. Allain was content to hold her granddaughter and let the rest of the family talk. She only added to the conversation when asked about the funeral service that would take place in two days.

David observed how Lamina and Kevin watched Allain with the baby. Allain had mentioned to him that she and Kevin had been talking about who would raise the baby. Since Kevin and Lamina wanted children she thought it would be a good idea to let them raise the baby. When Kevin got up to get a drink from the kitchen David followed him in. Allain had laid the baby down in the new room and went to change her clothes.

"Kevin have you talked to your mom about the baby?" David hadn't meant to launch right into the topic but the events of the past several weeks had left him deficient of small talk.

"No, and honestly we're afraid to. Mom is still mourning Shannon and to ask her if we could raise the baby as our own for some reason seems cruel to us. We really don't know what to do."

David placed a hand on the young man's shoulder unsure how or if he should proceed with giving out advice.

"Kevin, you mom, though she is hurting, needs to know the truth. If you let the situation extend longer and longer it will become more difficult for her to give the baby to you and Lamina." David had to work hard to keep his selfish, underlying reasons at bay. He wanted to take Allain away, far from the hurt and heartache. He saw the almost envious look Kevin and Lamina had and he knew they desired children. He didn't want to invade their personal situation but he also knew time was of the essence if Allain was going to begin the healing of her own heart.

"I know you're right. Maybe after the funeral? We could do it then." David had never seen Kevin with such doubt and worry.

"No, Kevin. We will all sleep here tonight and tomorrow, once you've all decided on a name for the baby you and Lamina will take her home."

Kevin had looked at him with horror at first and then as the words sunk in he nodded his agreement and they returned to the living room. Kevin whispered silently to Lamina and led her to the guest room. Jake had already retired to his old room and he knew Allain was sleeping in the same room with the baby. He situated himself on the couch not trusting himself to lay in Allain's bed, they'd have to run off to Las Vegas for sure.

He heard the baby cry a few hours later and watched as Allain changed her, fed her and put her back to bed. *I knew she could be a mom again but was she ready to give that job to someone else?* He knew that Allain's broken heart would not heal if she tried to fix her hurts by raising the baby. Even though he wasn't a parent and didn't know the depth of the hurt when one loses a child, he did understand grief and the deceptive way it could creep in and make a person make hasty decisions.

He knew in his heart that he would have to move quickly. If anything was left to linger it would bring more difficulty and struggle. Over the past months of getting to know Kevin and Lamina better he had learned that Lamina was unable to conceive a child. They had not voiced their hope that Allain would allow them to raise Shannon's baby. They didn't want to take the fragile link that seemed to keep Allain going.

After breakfast the newest member of the family was given the name Trinity Shannon Krisson. David marveled at how everyone took turns holding her and wished their own blessing for her.

When he and Allain had been alone he had broached the subject of Kevin and Lamina taking Trinity and she had become angry and resistant. He had patiently explained how this could work for all of them and she had kicked him out of her house.

Eventually Allain would come to see it was a great idea. She would have to work out the feelings of her betraying Shannon and not raising Trinity herself. David had simply stated that's where he comes in.

Chapter 17

Hearts will never be practical until they are made unbreakable... [Wizard of Oz]

Allain sat down heavily on the porch as the Salvation Army truck drove away. All of Shannon's clothing had been packed up and given away. Allain had kept a few knick knacks and collectibles and was glad to have gotten through the process. She wasn't quite ready to go back into the house. All the baby furniture had been moved over to Kevin's and little Trinity Shannon was bonding with them and thriving.

Allain knew in her heart that letting the baby go with Kevin and Lamina was the right thing to do but it still smarted. The anguish of losing Shannon was too close to the surface. She knew the baby wouldn't replace Shannon but it has provided a soothing balm while making all the funeral arrangements and dealing with the legal proceedings. David had been her champion, making sure things got done and she never had to check back about anything.

The day they had brought Trinity home had been bittersweet. The family had hunkered down at her house and David had seen to everyone's needs while she spent time with the baby. She briefly thought back to the night and morning before going to the hospital when she wanted David to make love to her. Allain put her hands on her cheeks as she recalled the battle they both fought as she laid in his arms. This was not how she had thought things would come together. They should have been some place exotic on their honeymoon not thinking about anyone or anything. Instead she had to make funeral arrangements and prepare for a newborn.

Allain was still fuming from the television exposé on the gunman. He was being portrayed as some modern day Robin Hood crusading for those who had been abused by the medical system's policy of handling patients and insurance company politics. She didn't agree when abortion doctors were murdered and she definitely wasn't going to agree with the loss of life that had ensued just because the gunman wasn't going to be able to get his way. She had called up the news program and voiced her disbelief at how the real victims were being disregarded. She did regret saying that maybe we all should kill when we can't get what we want.

She hadn't been angry with David when he left the room and told her to get ready. He had been right and she was grateful that they hadn't yielded. His support had been a major source of strength. He had come to her right from the airport. She shook her head as she remembered how angry he became when he saw her bandages. They had cried together when she took him to see Shannon. The steady heartbeat of her unborn grandchild had been the only other thing to keep her from going over the edge.

She had left the legal and court proceedings to Jake. Trinity was with Kevin and Lamina. She felt at a loss. She was on leave from the university and she knew she should be getting some rest but she just wanted to be busy so she wouldn't have to think. When Trinity had awoken for another feeding David had taken the baby to Lamina. Allain had been so weary she hadn't complained. He had come back into the living room, picked her up and taken her to her room, tucking her into her bed. He kissed her on the forehead like a child and then closed the door. Just knowing he was outside the door had given her such peace that she gave herself over the oblivion that sleep provided.

She had woken the next morning with a start but relaxed when she heard David's voice in the living room. He was telling Kevin to get home and get some rest. She was silently agreeing with him when her thoughts turned to Trinity. Allain had jumped out of bed and run out her bedroom. She saw Kevin heading out the door with a baby bag on his arm. Just as she was going to ask what was going on David had beat her to the punch. He softly said that they were going home to get some rest and would be back tomorrow to pick them up before the funeral. She had wanted to scream that they weren't going anywhere but David had pulled her back into the house while Kevin got into the car.

Allain turned accusatory eyes on him and released her anger. "You planned this didn't you? Get everyone out of the house so you could have me all to yourself. Poor vulnerable Allain. She is in need of someone to rescue her." She didn't want to hear his explanation about her needing to rest. She didn't want to accept the fact that the baby needed to go home with Lamina and Kevin. And David pointed out that they were not alone but that Jake was in the back room taking care of all the phone calls.

Allain had walked to the room that was supposed to have been Shannon's and Trinity's and noticed that many things had been moved out. The room felt so empty without the baby items in it and her heart felt that way as well.

She wanted to hit him, cuss him out, knock his brains in and kick him till she felt better. Her brain knew he had been right. If she had gotten her way, the baby may have never left her house and she'd be raising another baby. Her heart lashed back, this is your daughter's child. You have as much right as anyone. She knew she was going to say something harsh so she backed away from David's outstretched arms and went to her room. She lay in her bed unable to cry or move. Her thoughts were random and unorganized.

Who does he think he is? Was he the man of the house now? She had seen David command attention and speak with authority when warranted. Her sons were listening to him and coming to him for advice. For the first few weeks while they waited for Trinity's delivery date she hadn't minded. The boys needed a man to talk to and she couldn't have picked a better, more caring person other than her pastor. He had even come to her defense when she hadn't openly decided on what they should do about Trinity's care once she was born.

In private David had even given her counsel, telling her not to wait too long to decide. To be considerate of Kevin and Lamina's feelings and that they would need to bond with the baby as soon as possible. She had agreed but she had not really meant the words. Maybe that was why she had tried to seduce him on Trinity's birth date. She hadn't really meant that either, not completely.

She wanted a distraction; she wanted David to fuck her. She needed to escape from the pain and from the fear, anything to help her not think. Her body wanted to be violent and pushed to its limits. She didn't want gentle love making and soft caresses.

136

She wanted harsh abandon to consume her mind and help her forget. Again David knew that this temporary fix would not have been enough. After being celibate for so long reducing herself to fucking would have left her angry with herself.

She needed to deal with her fear. She would never feel comfortable in a hospital lobby ever again. Dealing with the fear had been put on the back burner because she needed to be at her daughter's side. Her anger at the gunman was something she knew she was going to have to work through but sitting at his trial was not going to prove a productive avenue for that either.

She had told the counselor, who was made available to all the survivors; she wanted to kill the gunman. She wanted to use the same crazed abandon he had used when he killed all those people. She knew those thoughts were there because she hadn't been praying. Her pray life was borderline flunking and she rationalized her status. She didn't want to offend God when she prayed because her prayers would be angry, cynical prayers. She wanted to give God an ear full and then some and she wanted to use words that she would never say and it scared her so much she decided she better put praying off for a while until she cooled down.

At the funeral service the pastor has spent a great deal of time with them. He basically acted like there was no one else in the sanctuary but them. He had really ministered to them and Allain had let go a great deal of anger and fear. She was even ready to accept that fact that God could handle all her emotions, purge her system and get her back to her right mind.

It had been easier to let Trinity go home with Kevin and Lamina that day. After talking to various family and friends she was glad for the quiet and peace that she and David found in each other's arms. Days blended into weeks but she just couldn't bring herself to go through Shannon's belongings. David had volunteered to help her, but she had let her anger rule and had told him that he could do all of it.

He had put his money where his mouth was and had done all the packaging. Of course some of it was easy since Shannon had just begun to move in with her. She watched in horror as he moved box after box into her garage. She had kicked him out that night. David had said that he would call her after she had cooled down. She immediately went to the garage and started to open the boxes but got ahold of herself and went back into the house. She went into Shannon's room and began to look around.

David had gone above and beyond yet again. On the bed he had left stuffed animals and dolls. Photo albums and items of a personal nature he had displayed on the bookcases. She fell to her knees and cried as she admired the care and detail he had paid to items she herself would have picked out to save for Trinity.

The next morning she had driven over to his place with a single rose to apologize. He took her into his arms and said they wouldn't speak of it again. After a filling breakfast of his trademark Australian pancakes they had went for drive. When the gas gauge had gotten to almost E they were half way to San Francisco.

"David I just feel so horrible about how I've taken all my angry feeling out on you. I know who I am supposed to be angry with but he's locked away where I can't strangle him. And I feel like I'm betraying Shannon with giving her things away and yes giving her baby away. I know Kevin is family but he's my son. I know I can see Trinity anytime I want but part of me just can't seem to get past it."

She smiled as David took her hand and let her talk. "You are too good for me, you know that. I'm keeping you from your work. I haven't seen paint on your hands or face in weeks."

She had nearly fallen out of the car when he said if he couldn't be there for the woman he loved than all the art and paint in the world couldn't fill the hole he'd have in his heart.

Shaking her head she couldn't believe she was in love with a man more romantic than she was.

"Well I guess there is only one thing left to do." David had looked at her with a quizzical look. "It is time to plan a wedding." She laughed the rest of the drive and David bounced in his seat like a child on his way to Disneyland.

Chapter 18

You are what I never knew I always wanted. [Fools Rush In]

David shook his head as his father adjusted his collar on his tuxedo for the hundredth time. "Dad you seem more nervous than me."

"Just making sure you look presentable to my future daughter. Can't have you looking like some bum off the street."

"I love you too dad," David said with a smile. His parents had flown in two months ago to spend time with their soon-to-be new daughter. He had felt his heart swell when his parents referred to her as one of their own. They never liked being called in-laws and refused to use it on anyone else. Even Regia had been called daughter.

The past two months had been the most joyous of his life and he knew that more joy was to come. He had been a little hurt when his parents invited Allain to events that he wasn't invited to. He had been pawned off on his sisters and their families, showing them the sites of Southern California. He felt ready to kidnap Allain and run off to Las Vegas if he had to go to one more amusement park or museum without her.

He had hoped to help Allain with the plans for their wedding and maybe provide some support when his mother wanted to usurp authority and start to run things. At the dinner one evening his father had pulled him aside and told him that he had nothing to fear. Allain had held her ground for what she wanted and "I think you mom is experiencing for the first time in her life not getting her way."

David laughed to himself as his mother fussed over Allain everywhere they went. When he had gotten a chance to stand next to Allain he had whispered in her ear what he suspected his parents' were up to. She had smiled mischievously up at him and whispered back that is was to generate more excitement for what's to come. His heart skipped a few beats as he saw the sparkle in her eyes.

Every day had become an adventure as David tried to steal a kiss or two from Allain. A week before the wedding his father had taken pity on them and planted his rental car keys in David's pocket. When Mrs. Haydon wasn't looking David and Allain had slipped off to spend time alone before the final rehearsal. They had driven over to the park and sat together on the same bench when they had first met. They kissed each other passionately, silently promising to bring much more. His mom had given them an earful later but it had been worth it. Everything went well at the final rehearsal and dinner with the family. Allain was happy with how things were coming together and that was enough for him.

He frowned remembering the not so nice phone calls and emails Allain had received after her impromptu television interview. She had been angry and hurt, justifiably so, but the horrible things that were being said, especially how doctors bring things like this on themselves really made him doubt humanity. Just because Shannon was a physician didn't mean she invited her own demise on herself. Not all doctors contribute to the growing health care problem at large. Where were the thinking people? David shook those thoughts away, satisfied that the gunman will be brought to justice no matter what reasons were given.

David was drawn out of his revelry by the pastor's knock on the door. "You ready young man?" David nodded, "Then its time, follow me."

"All right Dad let's go." They walked out of the pastor's office to the foyer of the sanctuary. He nodded to family and friends as they walked by. Received thumbs up from Brannon and a few other friends from the art world.

They entered from the left making their way to the front near the pulpit. After the rehearsal dinner he and Allain had kissed one final time and she and his sisters had kicked everyone out. He had learned later that they hadn't gotten back to her place until two in the morning.

Their efforts were breathtaking. Accenting every pillar were white and pale pink carnations. Each aisle of pews had white and pale roses with intertwined ribbons strung from pew to pew. The candle holder he had seen the night before had been redecorated with pink and white ribbons and the unity candle stand had been also decorated and their names added to it. The care and detail was indeed tremendous and David felt his heart brimming with love and appreciation for the woman of his dreams.

Kevin met him at the front and smiled. "I'm about ready to go get mom and walk her down the aisle to you. Any last requests? We can still have that bachelor party. Mom is probably not ready anyway, we've got time."

David laughed at Kevin and put his hand on his shoulder. "When I met you mom a year ago any female, especially a performer, lost any chance of getting my attention. You couldn't pay me to notice anyone."

Kevin nodded, "I am so glad that you two are going to make each other happy. There would be one more thing that would have made this day even more special but I know she's smiling down from heaven and she'll turn her head once you guys start the honeymoon."

Kevin looked away and let his eyes sober a little before continuing. "In all seriousness, all three of agreed that we wanted this for mom. Shannon had been resistant at first but that changed once she began to deal with her own heart issues. I know she is glad, as we all are that you both have found what you seek."

David smiled at the young man trying to play father and give him the blessing of the family. "I am so blessed to be entering into a family that genuinely cares for each other and looks out for one another. Now enough talking and go get your mother."

Kevin hugged him and proceeded to the back of the sanctuary. David glanced over at Lamina and Trinity, now a plump four month old. Trinity was happily examining her hands while Jake nodded to him that he knew that Kevin had given him the talk. Allain had brought a fullness he had never known into his life. He was a father and grandfather all in one day. He never would have thought it possible.

The orchestra continued to play softly in the background and found it ironic that they were getting married almost to the day when we they first met on their blind date. He had been determined to not cry at his own wedding, stating he needed a clear vision of everything that would happen today. But he knew he was going to lose that battle.

The music seemed to lift him back in time as he remember seeing her at the coffee shop, the look on her face as he approached her table and the horrified look she had when she "spit" her chocolate on him. Who would have known that after another food mishap and even his time away that they would finally get their act together and do what they should have done the first week. He reflected how beautiful she had been for the movie premier and how non-assuming when they picked out wedding rings. She had been gracious and poised as he introduced her to the sometimes over the top art world.

Each date was burned into his memory along with her smile at his weird jokes and tales from his childhood. She had a unique way of pouting when she wanted her way and she didn't realize when she was angry her eye brows would arch sharply and her hands would go to her hips. He was glad her anger had lessened as the trial for the gunman had progressed. He had wanted to forbid her from going. She had become consumed with the proceedings and had stopped eating. Having her go through Shannon's things had helped somewhat but this would be a wound that would never completely heal. His heart had broken each time she cried and if he had had the power he would have turned back time and put things back the way they were. She was giving the house to Jake who would need it as he started his ministry. They had moved most of her things to their new condo in the last few weeks and he couldn't wait till their home had her touches all over it and they christened each room with their love.

He chuckled to himself when she tried sushi for the first time and he tried chitlins. Allain was a wonderful cook and he knew that if they didn't start an exercise regimen soon he would be a fat Aussie. He knew she enjoyed teaching math but he wondered if she had also missed her calling as a chef. The family get-togethers had reminded him of picnics his family would take when he was a child. They had promised that they would continue to have the "kids" over eventually but there would be no hurry as they enjoyed newlyweddom.

He had learned to carry her spirit with him every day. It showed in his artwork but even when he approached his usual daily activities, he knew he was different. He thought he needed to talk to Regia and make things right but that had not been necessary at all. He had just needed to be honest with himself and realize who he was and what he wanted. He had never been especially religious but being a part of Allain's Christian family had brought a peace in his life that some years ago he would have thought impossible. He glanced at Pastor Patrick who nodded to the musicians.

He turned to face the audience and he waited for the wedding march to begin. When Kevin didn't appear with Allain he started up the aisle to the sitting room designated for her use. He had just entered the foyer when he heard what sounded like a gun shot.

Chapter 19

When you realize you want to spend the rest of your life with somebody, you want the rest of your life to start as soon as possible. [When Harry Met Sally]

Allain stood facing the full length mirror and exhaled slowly. She was so excited she was about to jump out of her skin. She was marrying the love of her life. This day would have been absolutely perfect if Shannon were here. Allain wrapped her arms around herself and squeezed. "Yes, sweetheart, I feel your love. I thank you for yours and your brothers blessing. Your daughter is such a jewel. She will know what a wonderful person you are."

Wiping the tears from her eyes and sat at the dresser and fixed her eye makeup. Her new mom had been most gracious helping her get dressed and her new sisters had even stood in as brides maids. Pushing her sadness aside she smiled as she thought back to all the work they did into the wee hours last night. Pale pink had been Shannon's favorite color and she had always loved carnations.

"Mom you're never going to get married, are you?" She remembered her precious fourteen year old asking her that. It was just after the kids had tried to fix her up with yet another teacher from school. "Someday I'll be with the person I'm supposed to be with if that's the way God wants it. For now I'm glad to have you and your brothers to keep me busy."

"Well, I hope God butts out of my love life. He takes too long." Allain hadn't known then how to answer her daughter. She had become content to not have to deal with the foolishness that sometimes came along with men and relationships.

"God does answer prayer, even if the answer isn't always what we are expecting or wanting." Her thoughts went to David and the unexpectedness that came with their relationship. Hard to believe that so much had happened in a year's time since they had met.

Fingering her diamond solitaire she felt lightness in her heart as she remembered how he proposed and the way he had looked into her eyes as he told her how much he loved her. She laughed as she thought about how her coworkers had started to fall over themselves to have David come up to the campus. They ulterior motive was to get his father to come for a visit but it had been entertaining to see people that call themselves professional act like star struck teenagers. The reception should be very interesting. "I wonder who will trip over themselves first in front of Mr. Haydon."

The knock on the door woke her from her thoughts. "Kevin, you're right on time." Taking another look at herself in the mirror she opened the door to let him in. "Come on in sweetheart, let me get my bouquet. So, you ready to...." she swallowed the words as she looked in the face an angry woman holding a gun.

"That's your sweetheart I left unconscious out there? My sweetheart will never grow up like yours, especially given what he daddy did. What you've nothing to say. You're all fired up about the victims, I thought it be fitting to let you know about the one you forgot."

Allain gripped her bouquet trying to stay composed. She silently thanked God that Kevin was still alive. There was no way that she could make it out the door. She stood facing the woman that seemed to only have deadly intent on her mind.

"You know it was hard tracking you down. You stopped coming to court. I assumed you were holed up with your little boyfriend somewhere. Then just by chance I happened to be looking through the newspaper. You see there isn't much to do when you're waiting all day at the court. And splat there you were. All gussied up and smiling. What you got to smile about, didn't you lose someone recently?"

Allain tried to keep her anger and grief veiled as she regarded the woman standing across from her. To look at her, one would never have thought that she had come mentally unglued. Maybe it was more than that, she was no psychologist but she didn't think this was a planned attack, more of a desperate call to be heard.

Allain watched in horror as the woman fired the gun up at the ceiling. "I asked you a question. Don't think about trying to get outta here. You'll leave here when and how I want you to leave here."

Allain didn't like the sound of that but she was not going to lose her cool. She sat down in the nearest chair in the parlor and answered, "It was my daughter who was shot that day."

"A daughter. I'll never know the pleasure."

"Neither will I, since she is dead." Allain wasn't given a chance to feel satisfied as the woman rushed up to her face and sneered at her

"Don't try to compare your pain to mine. Your daughter was a doctor and as far as I'm concerned she was just as guilty. Don't look at me like that. Doctors like money and if they aren't going to get it than you're not worthy of the lint off their jacket."

"Believe me I understand the frustration. While raising my children I had my own run-ins with insurance companies and arrogant doctors, I can assure you…"

"You can't assure me of anything. I have had enough of sympathy and pats on the back that things will get better. My son is going to die and there is nothing anyone can do. Yes my son, the real victim in all this."

"Why don't you sit down and tell me. *Think fast Allain, keep her talking.* What is your name?"

Allain had noticed the woman's hand had begun to shake and seemed to start sweating profusely.

"Don't think being nice to me is going to change anything. I mean to prove my point."

"I believe you. I'm the bride and I can be as late as I want to be for my own wedding, to a certain degree. I'm not sure if proving your point to me will be helpful to what you want to achieve, but I will listen." Allain couldn't believe her calm. David you must be praying, just don't come through the door.

"What should I call you?" Allain asked again.

"My name is Melissa and I going to tell you about the victim you forgot. Now I don't agree with how my husband took matters into his own hands. I wept when I read how many people died but no one would listen. Our son had been suffering for months before we finally found someone that would listen and at least diagnosis the problem. We didn't ask for unemployment. We didn't 'not' want to have insurance. We sold everything to keep the treatments going once we learned what he had. It was completely curable but you had to pay for the cure. We had nothing left and we couldn't continue the treatments."

Melissa got a faraway look. "I started to do things I never thought I would do just to get money. You would have thought I was a drug addict if I told you

151

about the things I lowered myself to do. And I did anything and everything so my son could get treatment. But it wasn't enough. My husband really did lose his mind. He couldn't deal with the pain our son was enduring. He stopped visiting and he couldn't bear to look at me anymore." Melissa turned to face Allain fully.

"I don't know where he got the gun but seeing myself holding one I now know how easy it is to get one. What do you say to that Ms. Victim's Advocate?" Melissa was pointing the gun at Allain demanding she answer.

"What was done to your son was indeed horrible, but killing innocent people isn't going to win people to your cause. Did you know my daughter was part of the group Doctors Without Borders? She joined right out of medical school. She believed in all people having the right to medical care. Not all doctors are caught up in themselves. There are those who really want to help people. Your husband took the law into his own hands."

"Well isn't that what you advocated. Kill if we can't get what we want."

"I was angry. My daughter had been ripped away from me and my grandchild had been put at risk. I felt that your husband needed to die. No reason or excuse would ever condone what he did. I know you are the one holding the gun but more people will side with how I feel than how you feel. Killing a person won't bring back the one you love and it won't make the pain go away. I had to learn that. How I view you husband is immaterial. You still have a son that needs at least one of his parents. Don't waste your chance to still make a difference.

"Allain!" Both women jumped at the bellow outside the door. "David, don't come in, I'm alright. See to Kevin."

Allain faced Melissa and continued, "Melissa, I am sorry for my angry words but there has got to be something that can be done, somewhere your son can be taken."

"Allain tell her I'll pay for it. As long as no harm comes to you or anyone else I'll take care of everything." David yelled through the door.

"Melissa, please put the gun down. You don't want to do this and I know there is somewhere else you'd rather be. Where is your son right now?"

Melissa answered with a sob, "He's still in the hospital but they only do the minimal for him and nothing more."

"Allain have her tell me which hospital, I'll call right now." Allain could hear the desperation in David's voice and was hoping that her calm was getting through to Melissa.

"What? Wait a minute, you're trying to trick me, you're calling the police." Melissa began to move toward the door.

David slipped inside with his hands up. "I promise you I have no intention of calling the police. Just tell me what hospital your son is in and you'll be free to go, minus your friend here."

Allain's heart had moved to her throat and she could hardly breathe. David met her eyes and she drew strength from his resolve.

Melissa had lowered the gun but not released it. "I don't understand. What are you people really after? All I want is my son to get well."

Allain's eyes never left David's, "then tell use the hospital you son is in, let us help you."

"Mom!" Allain heard Kevin shout.

"I'm alright. Go tell everyone we will start in twenty minutes. Tell them not to leave the sanctuary. Don't ask any questions just do it."

Melissa's hands began to shake more as she looked from Allain to David. "You're only doing this out of fear. If I didn't have a gun you would have had me removed from the building."

"Melissa do you want our help or not? We'll call the hospital, go into the church and get married and then you can slip out of the building without any hindrance. Do you want your son or do you want to prove a point?" David had inched closer to Allain to be a shield if he needed to.

Melissa put the gun down and let the tears flow freely. "I am so sorry. I can't let you do this. I have to find another way, a right way." She put her hand up to stall their objections. "No I mean it, leave me, please don't make me pick up this gun again. Go I've held you up long enough."

David stepped over to Allain offering his hand as she stood. She knew her eyes mirrored the relief she saw in his eyes. They locked at the woman who had seemed to shrunken in the last five minutes but had a new determination about her. She nodded at them as they opened the parlor door. David stepped aside while Allain walked out. He closed the door quickly coming face to face with Kevin, Mr. Haydon and the Pastor.

"We're ready!" they said in unison.

Chapter 20

This kind of certainty comes, but once in a lifetime [Bridges of Madison County]

David had been reluctant to let her go as she stood at the back of the church and he went to the front with his father. His heart swelled anew as Kevin walked her down the aisle to him. They had given a hasty explanation for the delay, something about Kevin bumping his head and knocking some things over. They had finally gotten everyone settled down and ready for the ceremony thirty minutes after the mysterious sound that had shook the church.

David told Jake about the "item" that needed disposing of and Jake had made a quick call to a friend. His friend, a sergeant Jeff, had swung by and taken care of things. He shook off the anger that had risen in him. Nodding to Kevin he took Allain's hand in his and they faced the pastor.

She squeezed his hand back, reassuring him that she was fine and that they had done the right thing. They soon forgot about everyone else as they said their vows and exchanged rings. The eternity was over as the pastor announced them a husband and wife.

David pulled her into his arms and held her gaze for the briefest of seconds before he lips descended on hers. Time seemed to disappear as he kissed his wife with such tenderness, relishing her sigh against his mouth. He released her as the applause and claps got louder. Smiling, they walked down the aisle arm and arm.

***

"I'd like to make a toast," began Kevin. "When I first met my mom, I didn't know what to make of her. We got along pretty ok, I believe those were the words I used to use, and for the most part we didn't have much trouble. But she was sure stubborn. Each time my brother, sister and I would bring her someone to marry; she always found a way to thwart our efforts. I heard her once tell my sister that when she did give her heart it would be completely without any reservations. Mom was waiting for the person she was supposed to be with, the best and I'm glad that I was able to finally bring home the right one."

Kevin waited for the laughter and claps to quiet down. "To my mom's husband, the man I always knew as Mr. Too Sexy, at least that's what all the ladies at work called him. I liked him the first moment I met him. He carries such intensity about everything he works on that I know he will take special care with details and anything most precious to him. I didn't know when I set them up on a blind date that not only were their wishes going to come true but mine and my siblings as well. May you both continue to love completely and with such intensity that each day will be sweeter and every level will get better. I know I speak for Jake, Shannon and myself when I say we are so blessed to have these two wonderful people as part of our family. To Mr. and Mrs. Hayden I know God will bless you forever"

Allain stood and hugged her son. She then proceeded to give a toast of her own, thanking her children for their endless antics, for blessing her with a beautiful daughter in-law and precious granddaughter. She had basically given up on being a married person. She was resolved to just be content with the victories her children would win and be a loving grandmother when the time came for it. She had only relented to the "blind date" because she was tired of the whining and the pitiful performance her children kept rendering. They were getting too old for such behavior and she was hoping that this would be the stop of it. Well it had. David is everything and more than she prayed for and she was glad that they would be on this journey together.

There wasn't a dry eye when she finished and kissed David causing the hoots and hollers to begin again.

David rose, clearing his throat, "If I'd know there was all this talking and syrupy speeches I'd have kidnapped my jewel weeks ago and you'd all might be getting postcards about our whereabouts. Of course I shouldn't have expected anything less when our first meeting seemed to always end in a food or beverage mishaps. I pray we don't fall into the cake." He paused to give Brannon a dirty look for trying to make an indecent suggestion saying there was still time. "There are days I feel like I've known Allain all my life. Everything about her brings joy to my life. I pray that God will make me into the husband I am to be to you. To share in your joys, kiss away your tears and shoulder your burdens as we begin this wonderful journey. May I always be worthy of you." After kissing her he led her to the dance floor and they danced their first dance.

The night seemed to drag by but they continued to enjoy their family and friends. Hours later and a wardrobe change Jake dropped them off at LAX. Allain had been a little disappointed that they weren't staying at least one night together before leaving for their trip, especially since it was such a late hour. David had promised he'd make it up to her, especially since this had been not only a long day but a very trying one as well. He knew that if they had gone back to their home they would not have made the flight the next morning. She soon began to get excited when she learned they were leaving for Aruba and wouldn't be back for three weeks.

They talked quietly about Melissa and her situation. David had been ready to do whatever it took to ensure Allain's safety. Allain had said she still wasn't completely sure how she felt about the entire incident. She was going to need time to think about it and then she'd make plans to do something to help all victims on all sides. She didn't say more and he didn't push for more. They snuggled as much as they could in their airplane seats and let their thoughts turn to their honeymoon.

One week later

David leaned back on the pillows and gazed toward the balcony window. He had never felt so at peace. He was content to just spend the rest of their days in their room. He smiled as he heard the rumblings in the bathroom. His bride was determined to leave the room today and do some shopping.

"Honey don't you want to come back to bed? I've got something for you," He ducked as she threw a pillow at him. "Come on have a little mercy on a man in love."

Allain paused for a brief moment remembering all the "loving" they had done. She smiled as she and David had basically badgered the taxi driver to hurry up and get them to their hotel. The manager had quickly checked them in and the bell hop had not dawdled after bringing them to the room and unloading their luggage.

David had taken her in his arms as soon as the door had closed. His intense kiss had left her breathless and wanting more. Soon their hands were speaking languages only the body parts they touched could understand.

Allain shivered as his hand slid inside her shirt and eased it up and over her head. He continued to nuzzle her neck as she ran her hands up and down his arms. She felt her bra come undone and tingled with anticipation as he removed the straps.

"You're so beautiful. I don't think we're going to make it to the bed." David was trying to slow down his breathing but his heart rate was not cooperating. He pulled her to him crushing her in another searing kiss, loving the feel of her breasts on his chest. He moved to her neck as he pushed her skirt to the floor. He felt the lace of her panties and knew she had worn something sexy just for him. He reached inside to touch her core and watched her eyes darken even more with passion. "Allain, look at me. Tell me what you want because I know once I get started I won't be able to have a rational thought any longer." He began to quicken his ministrations, relishing as her body responded to his touch.

"David you have on too many clothes. I need you now." Allain rasped out as her eyes closed against his gentle and insistent assault. She whimpered slightly as he removed his hand and she watched him removed his shirt, shorts then underwear. She unconsciously licked her lips as she watched his manhood strain toward her.

"Allain…" David began as he pulled her to him and pushed her up against the wall. He wanted to slow down, he knew it had been some time since she had been intimate with anyone but the looks she was giving him where going to send him over the edge. He left her neck and traveled to the valley between her breasts. He massaged her nipples until he felt her scratch his shoulders. His kissed one breast and continued massaging the other while returning his free hand to her core. He was going to make sure she was ready for him, even if he died first.

He kneeled before her and continued to trail kissed down her stomach, coming just above the junction at her thighs. He heard her catch her breath and looked at him. "Allain I am going to love you all over and make sure you are ready for me."

She barely got a nod out as she felt his breath on her center. Her heart was slamming against her chest in anticipation as he lifted her left leg and placed it on his shoulder. At the first touch of his tongue on her center she was thankful to be leaning against the wall because she surely would have fallen. She put her finger in her mouth to keep from screaming. She felt David chuckle as he continue to drive her insane. Never had a lover taken such care and gentleness when touching her body.

David was becoming drunk with her taste and he felt her climax against his mouth, he continued his torture until her spasms ceased. He kissed his way back up her body to her lips and gently lifted her in his arms. He slipped into her easily and rested his head in the curve of her neck until she gave him a sign to start to move.

He didn't have to wait long. Allain had tasted herself on his lips and it had reignited her speeding heart. She wiggled slightly while holding on to his shoulders, trying to draw him deeper if at all possible.

David needed no further persuading as he began to thrust into her long and hard. He would almost withdrawal out of her completely, driving her wild, as he tried to prolong their love making. She soon climaxed again and he followed soon after. They stayed against the wall trying to catch their breath a moment longer.

"I love you so much. I knew from the moment I met you, you would complete me." David's words had brought tears to her eyes, which he quickly kissed away. He walked to the couch and laid her there. He smiled as she began to pout, kissing her quickly, "I'll be right back, I'm going to put the 'Do Not Disturb' sign on the door and lock all the locks."

By the time he finished he was ready for her again. They spent the entire night christening the living room of their suite. They would make it to the bed by the next day and they would not leave the room for the next seven days.

Coming back to the present she put on her shades, smiling to herself. She told him that he had one hour to meet her in the lobby after she finished her breakfast at the hotel restaurant. After that he'd be on his own. He jumped out of the bed as she got to the door. He shamefully paraded his nudity in front of her. She laughed and ran out of the room as he gave one last attempt to tempt her back to bed.

Well old man I guess we're going to have to do better to keep our woman in check. He made haste and got himself ready for a day among the throngs of tourists with his beautiful wife.

It was a balmy eighty degrees in Aruba and David smiled as Allain stepped into every shop and just couldn't say no to the street vendors. She had whispered in his ear that she had to make up for lost time. Of course he didn't recall any complaints as they made love. He had only nodded but he knew she had enjoyed being lost in each other's arms.

He grinned to himself remember how insatiable his wife was. When the airplane had landed they were glad to get their luggage and get to their hotel room with no problems. He had barely tipped the room attendant when his wife attacked him. Everything was forgotten as they were soon in each other's arms. Hurricane Allain had conquered him completely and he was more than willing to give himself over to the power of her assault.

David had hoped to go slowly and use the time to learn her skin and bring them to the brink of paradise. He also knew it has been some time since she had had sex and didn't want to hurt her. Allain was having none of it, she gave as strongly as she took and he found her exuberance intoxicating. By the fourth time they finally found the bedroom and the bed.

He shook his head as he remembered how the room service they ordered had "accidentally" landed on his stomach as was inching lower and she took her time offering assistance. His laugh soon turned to labored breathing when he saw the desire in her eyes. Of course her assistance had turned into more love making and a forgotten breakfast.

He would get his turn to have a little food fight as well. She had just gotten out of the shower and he was helping towel her hair when things got accelerated. He couldn't get enough of touching and kissing her. She'll never be able to look at Jell-O, whipped cream and chocolate syrup without blushing. It meant another trip to the shower and this time she didn't go alone. Better stop that train of thought or they may have to head back to the hotel room now.

They had lost all track of time over the past seven days and David had been ready to spend the next fourteen the same way. The Do Not Disturb Sign had become a permanent fixture on their door. It would not surprise him if the hotel staff ignored their room while they were out, though they had been most efficient when David had requested everything from towels to pillows.

David adjusted to going out of their hotel room as their days spent sightseeing gave way to passion filled nights. They had toured the Alto Vista Chapel, the California Lighthouse and the Frenchman's Pass. Then they had been in awe of the Ayo and Casibari Rock Formations and the Qua Dinky Caves.

While he had climbed Mount Jamanota, she had visited the Natural Bridge and Natural Pool. During their last week Allain spent time in the Aruba Aloe Factory and in Lourdes Grotto. They enjoyed the beaches and each sunset. Relishing how the simplest enjoyment resulted in passionate love making.

On their final night in Aruba they were content just being in each other's arms. He kissed her gently and whispered how much he loved her. Allain sat back against his chest and held his hand in hers. "I was so afraid and angry. My thoughts were all over the place. Where was Kevin? Was he alright? Had she done anything inside the sanctuary? Why was this happening to us and on our wedding day? My fear soon turned to disbelief. What did she think she was going to accomplish by attacking me? I lost my daughter that day. All the victims lost someone that day." She turned slightly to rest her head on his chest.

"I know I was angry, totally pissed off when I called in to the news program. I truly felt if he wanted to get some action he should have shot up the insurance office or held the CEO at gunpoint not the hospital. I feel so terrible for saying that. Since calming down I realize as a parent I would do almost anything to protect my children and I am thankful that I have never been in a situation where it seemed all hope was lost. I have thanked God everyday we've been here that everything turned out alright. So many things could have gone terribly wrong that day." She turned to look at him and saw his thoughts mirrored her own.

"Part of me wants to lock her away so she won't be tempted to hurt anyone else, but the more I thought about it the more I realized that that doesn't take away her hurt and the suffering she has had to endure. I was thinking we could start a foundation, the Shannon Foundation, and we could help families in need. We could provide education, professional counseling, financial assistance and whatever else is needed. Maybe this could help change the way insurance companies do business? I don't know I just want Shannon to be remembered for being a great doctor who carried about people and not just some statistic."

David looked into her eyes, saw her tears and pulled her even closer. He told her of how afraid he was when he heard the gun shot. He was thankful that most of the guests didn't hear it or recognize the sound. He had feared that he was going to lose her just when it seemed their time to be together had arrived. He let the tears drop from his eyes and felt his heart constrict at the thought of losing her. He couldn't say anymore, he let his gentle caressing and love making say it all. They fell asleep in the moon light after renewing their promise to forever love each other.

Chapter 21

"A life without love is no life at all." - Ever After: A Cinderella Story

David had laughed at how large Allain's eyes had gotten when she saw the enormous tip he left for the hotel staff. He had merely shrugged as they left the room. It had been worth it. Anything that they had needed the staff had provided. David put the additional suitcase with their entourage of others. She must have gotten a gift for everyone.

They road to the airport in silence, savoring the past three weeks. David wished it was December. He would have surprised her with a flight to Australia for the summer. He knew he would not be able to do it this Christmas, with it being Trinity's first Christmas, unless he flew the entire family over. He'd have to give it some more thought.

He felt her looking at him. "You're planning something." It wasn't a question. He tried to look innocent but just dazzled her with his handsome grin.

"I'm your husband, I'm supposed to be planning things." She laughed as he wiggled his eyebrows.

Jake picked them up at LAX and dropped them off at their condo. David busied himself with opening up the house while she and Jake caught up. An hour later they were alone with luggage on one side of the living room and wedding gifts on the other and their wedding photos and DVD was on the dining room table for them to view.

Allain was standing with her hands on her hips trying to decide which side of the room they should tackle first. David smiled at his organizer-bunny wife. It was two in the morning though they were still on Aruba time and it seemed like five a.m., this was not the time for laundry and opening presents.

David put his arms around her and kissed her. Once she was breathless he picked her up and carried her into the bedroom. Whispering in her ear, "We'll have the rest of our lives to do laundry and sign thank you card for our gifts. It's time to christen the bedroom and I won't take no for an answer."

Two months later

Allain was happy to retreat to the quiet of her office. The start of a new semester was always a challenge but for some reason she wasn't feeling as energetic as she usually would. It had been a long week and she was thankful that it was Friday and she could go home and relax. A headache seemed to be her constant companion of late. She was teaching three classes this semester and had started an outline for her new algebra book. Allain chalked it up to a full, stressful calendar.

She had to wake up an extra thirty minutes just to get rolling. David had said she was suffering from post-honeymoon syndrome, PHS. It was true she hadn't wanted to go back to work and was a little jealous of David's new stay at home job. He had gone per Diem with Videxel and was now back to painting full time. He was currently contemplating teaching a class at the university.

Taking some Tylenol she made her way to her car and the long drive home. She turned to happy thoughts as she looked forward to the meeting with Jake and some of the members from church that would be putting the Shannon Foundation together. Everything was starting to fall into place.

Trinity was growing like a weed and Lamina and Kevin were thinking in a year or two of adopting a brother for her. Allain smiled at the thought, remembering each day she brought her three wonderful children home. Adoption had been such a blessing, even if at times she didn't always think so. David would have made a great dad. His caring nature and attentiveness at times made her wish they were 5 or 10 years younger.

Allain didn't remember parking or taking the elevator up to the condo. She walked in and smelled something wonderful in the kitchen. David had been experimenting in the kitchen and she knew whatever it was she'd enjoy it. She walked past the living room and peeked in through the open door as David worked. She usually would watch him but she just felt extra tired all of a sudden. She went into their bedroom, stripped her outer clothes off and got into bed. Turning off the light, her last thought was just a little nap before dinner.

***

David heard Allain come in but didn't turn around when she paused at his open door. He was hoping she'd come in like she usually did so he could show her what he'd been up to all day. He knew the house smelled good, he'd been working on he's latest creation, an Australian twist to her gumbo.

He continued working for another hour and decided to go check on Allain. He didn't see her in the living room or kitchen and was a little surprised to not see her sitting at her desk. He looked in the bedroom and saw her clothes on the floor. With a smile he eased out of his clothes and slid into bed behind her, spooning up against her.

He touched her and noticed how warm she was. He pulled back the blankets and saw she had on just her underwear but was sweating profusely. "Allain, honey wake up. You're burning up." She turned her head toward his voice and slowly opened her eyes.

"I feel terrible." She said weakly and started to close her eyes again.

David jumped out of bed and ran into the bathroom to get a cool towel for her brow. Kneeling by the side of the bed he put the compress to her forehead.

"What can I do? Do you want to go to emergency?" He tried to keep the growing panic out of his voice but he had never seen her sick and he was unsure of what to do.

"No, I think I must be catching the flu. Those darn students, doesn't anyone stay home when they are sick anymore?" She tried to smile but felt like it would take too much energy. "I just need to rest and then I'll be right as rain."

David wasn't so sure but he decided not to argue. "Alright, I'll let you rest and I'll bring you something to eat in a little while." She nodded and turned over. As he closed the door he heard her say, "Nice outfit."

Three days later Allain finally got out of bed. David had about looked at every website trying to diagnose her symptoms. Most said to rest and stay hydrated. He knew that if she didn't get up by Monday he was taking her to emergency whether she wanted to go or not. She had only eaten his "gumbo" all weekend, saying it was a good thing he had forgotten to put the spices in otherwise she wasn't sure she'd be able to keep it down.

Thankfully Monday was Labor Day and the university was closed for the holiday. She was at her computer answering email when he checked in on her. "How ya feeling?"

She glanced up from the computer and smiled. "Much better. I'm actually a little hungry…what's for breakfast?"

"I could make you my world famous pancakes," he said as he walked over to her taking her into his arms. "Or we could get creative in the kitchen."

"Hey I just got my strength back and you want to take it all away already?" Allain said with a smile.

"My wonder woman wife hasn't got all her strength back yet?" David asked with a crocked smile. He led her into the kitchen and directed her to sit in one of the kitchen chairs while he prepared to cook. "I was a bit worried. I've never seen you sick before and I felt so helpless."

"Baby you did fine. Kept me comfortable and fed while I rested. I told you all I needed was rest and see I'm back on my feet." She suppressed a grin at her words knowing David wanted her off her feet and in an entirely different position. Changing subjects, "What kept you busy in your studio these past few days?"

"Oh, nothing much. I couldn't concentrate since I had to play nurse maid for an ailing damsel in distress." He began to crack the eggs open and add them to his pancake mix.

"Oh, brother! You better never get sick because I'll never let you live it down." She said getting up to set the table and taking the syrup from the cabinet. As she was pulling the silverware from the drawer she felt the room spin slightly and sat down rather quickly. *I must still be weak; I had better take it easy today.*

David turned back to her and saw her sitting, "Are you sure you're alright?"

"Hmm, oh yes. I think I'm still weak. You better feed me before I faint away from starvation." Kissing her on the cheek he went back to making pancakes.

After breakfast they reclined on the couch and watched a little television. Sighing with contentment she turned and looked in his eyes, "You are entirely too good for me. Even though I didn't eat much these last three days, I swear I am putting on weight with all your Aussie cooking."

"Well you know I like having something to hold on to," he said as he reached for her robe and drew her to him. He had meant to kiss her gently but her sigh made him add more urgency to the kiss. Just as he was to turn her so she was beneath him, her eyes got large and she jumped from the couch and ran to the bathroom. His lust was all forgotten as he ran after her and heard her retch up her entire breakfast.

Chapter 22

I've loved you from the moment I first laid eyes on you.
—Little Women

Allain waited on the line to talk to a nurse. She couldn't remember a time when she'd ever gotten so sick. She'd had the flu before but had never lost the contents of her stomach. She was feeling better but she knew she had to make this call or David would drive her to emergency. He had all but picked her up and put her in the car once she was able to leave the bathroom. By twelve o'clock she was able to eat some of his leftover gumbo with no problem. David had begun to suspect something might have been wrong with his pancake batter but she had started to feel ill again thirty minutes after they ate lunch but not with the same results.

Hello, I am Nurse Sharon. Could you tell me your full name and address?

Allain rattled off the information and waited for the next question.

Please describe your symptoms

Allain explained how she had been feeling fatigued, lacking her usual energy level. Otherwise she had felt fine.

For how many days? Fever? Diarrhea or constipation?

Three days, no fever, no diarrhea or constipation that she noticed.

When was your last menstrual period?

My last period? I actually don't know. I recently got married a little over two months ago and the fall semester just started back up at school. I don't think I've had a period since June. With my honeymoon and getting settled into my new place I just hadn't thought about it. *Oh my goodness…*

Allain couldn't finish her thought. She didn't even want to begin to hope and yet…

Mrs. Haydon, I can schedule you to come in and take a pregnancy test. You can be seen in urgent care at three-thirty this afternoon.

Allain vaguely remembers her saying okay we'll be there before hanging up the phone.

Could I actually be pregnant? Her emotions and feelings were all in a jumble. She thought she was done raising children. She was now a grandmother, her grandchild would be older than her aunt or uncle, if she was indeed pregnant. Maybe this was just menopause. That's what it had to be. Some women began the change as early as thirty-five years of age.

David came in and she shook herself from her musings. "What did they say?"

"I have an appointment for three-thirty this afternoon," not meeting his eyes. What was she going to say? She had always figured that they couldn't have children and had not pursued the subject any further. But now, all the what-ifs began to surface. She felt him sit down next to her on the bed.

Taking her hand, "Was there anything else they said?"

"No, they just feel I need to take some tests and then we can go from there." She couldn't tell him what kinds of tests. She still didn't quite believe it herself.

After getting dressed and trying not to spend too much time staring at her stomach they made the drive to the medical center. She kept her seat back and her eyes closed not trusting herself to speak. David reached over and held her hand as he drove. "I am sure it's nothing serious. I'm sorry I was so insistent that you go to the doctor. Everything is going to be fine."

Allain smiled knowing he was saying all this for his benefit as well as hers. After parking and checking in with reception they began the wait. She was called up only once to take a clear cup to the lab bathroom where she was instructed to leave her sample in the special window for the technician to retrieve.

Twenty-five minutes later the nurse called them back to an examination room. Allain was asked to take off all her clothing including her underwear and to put on a hospital gown. The nurse left them alone and Allain began to undress. She was all of a sudden feeling afraid and excited. She sat on the examination table and tried to calm her breathing.

David stood and took his wife in his arms. He was nervous too and was silently praying that she did not have a serious illness. Allain took comfort in his strength and tried not to think about what was going to happen next. She was just preparing to tell him that one of the tests she took was a pregnancy test when the doctor walked in.

Good afternoon folks. How are you both doing today?

They murmured the appropriate responses, looking at him apprehensively.

Well the results of your test are in. it is positive and we'll take a look and see how things are progressing.

David looked at the doctor with a puzzled look, "Positive for what doctor? Is it serious or…" he couldn't finish.

Oh I'm sorry. Your wife took a pregnancy test and she is pregnant. We want to see how far along she is since her last period was over two months ago.

178

David felt Allain looking at him and turned her taking her face in his hands. "Is this true?"

Allain shrugged, "I am just as surprised as you. I truly thought I had the flu. I would still think that if the doctor hadn't said differently."

The doctor instructed her to lie back and relax while the nurse prepared the ultrasound machine. The doctor examined her breasts and abdomen and told her to relax and he placed a condom over the probe and applied K-Y jelly to the top of the unit.

Take a deep breath Mrs. Haydon. You'll feel just a little pressure.

As the doctor inserted the probe all eyes turned to the screen and waited. He turned the probe this way and that and soon a small blip appeared on the screen. As the doctor got the angle he wanted, the little heart rate monitor began to register faster than they could count. David didn't notice the moisture that had gathered in his eyes as he saw their baby for the first time.

Their baby. He turned to Allain and kissed her. "Beautiful," was all he managed to get out as his voice broke with emotion.

You're doing good. Now let's take a look on the other side. Good, looks like the babies are about eight weeks and you can expect to deliver some time in late April. We will start you on prenatal vitamins and schedule an amniocentesis. You are an older first time mom and we want your pregnancy to be as little problematic as possible.

Allain let the tears flow freely as David gazed down at her with a heart full of love and emotion. Her head was swimming as she tried to focus on what the doctor was telling her.

Later that night as she laid in David's arms she silently thanked God for this unexpected blessing. David had spent hours on the phone with his family and they were looking forward to when they could all be together to meet the newest members of the family. Her children had taken the news well and were looking forward to their new siblings. This was one of those times when she wished that Shannon and Mari were here. Never in her life would she have thought that so many wonderful blessings would hit her at once.

She gazed at her sleeping husband and felt her heart swell with love and peace. She let the 'What-Ifs' leave her mind and strived to just enjoy the next eight months to come. David had promised that if she felt up to it they would go house hunting.

"If you don't stop looking at me that way I'm going to make love to you and see if we can make quadruplets." David eased up on his side to gaze down at her.

"I was just thinking how much I love you and how blessed I am," Allain sighed. She felt she better wait a while to prepare him for all the work that was to come. It had been a while since her children were babies and excited as she was for the adventure back into parenthood she knew this experience would be challenging.

As if reading her mind David ran his hand across her cheek, "If there is anything I've learned in the past year, it's that our love can indeed conquer all. And there isn't anyone I would rather be taking this journey with other than you. I feel like I could raise dozens of children with you at my side." David chuckled at her startled expression. "No, I don't think we need to go there, but it would be fun pretending." He began to kiss her and deepened the kiss as she moaned into his mouth.

David slowly began to unbutton her night shirt. He gently massaged her shoulders and then her breasts. He felt her relax under his touch. He replaced his hands with his mouth and enjoyed the sounds that came from deep in the back of her throat. He continued kissing a trail lower pausing at her abdomen. He kissed first the left side then the right whispering 'I love you' after each kiss.

Allain let her vision blur as the tears fell unhindered from her eyes. His gentle love making would forever repeat in her heart. She watched as he kissed his way back up her body to her lips and re-buttoned her shirt. He turned her away from him and drew her back up against him. She fell asleep to him kissing her neck, feeling the most loved in the world.

Eight months later

David stood by the bed in awe as Allain tried to get their daughter to latch on. He lifted his son to his shoulder whispering that his sister was being stubborn. His son seemed to grunt his agreement and drifted off to sleep.

David sat down in the rocking chair and transferred his son to his arm. Christopher Alex opened one eye briefly before settling back into sleep. Allain had labored for ten hours before their twins made their appearance. David smiled as he remembered how determined Allain was to have a vaginal delivery, and the kids were determined to make things happen before the scheduled cesarean section the following day.

He turned and watched Mira Christina finally latch on and Allain whisper, "You have no one to blame but yourself. You came out first but decided to make "eyes" at your daddy. You are going to have to accept that sometimes you are going to follow your brother, but I will always have enough for you both."

Allain looked up to see David smiling at her lopsidedly. She blew him a kiss with her free hand and beckoned him closer. David rose and came to sit on the side of the bed facing her and their daughter.

"Look what we've done." Allain beamed with joy in her voice. David thought she was the sexiest woman alive. "Don't look at me like that; I think these two are enough."

"For now," David said in his serious voice. Allain just shook her head and David laughed. "No you're right I don't want too many teen-agers in my retirement years."

"Now that they're here, I am so nervous. Once Kevin, Shannon and Jake had moved out I felt like I was done parenting. I had over the years thought about what I would have done differently but at this moment I am at a loss. I hope it will all come back with time."

"I know it will. I may not have been a parent before but I was actively involved in my nieces and nephews lives. We won't be perfect but will have enough love to make sure our children grow up cherished and cared for." David placed Christopher by his sister in the bassinet and sat back next to Allain drawing her in his arms.

"I knew I wanted to be with you for the rest of my life after meeting you at the coffee shop. Never could I have imagined the overwhelming joy I would receive. Almost makes me wish I had married you on the spot." David reached down and brought her hand to his lips.

Allain laughed, "Even after I spit at you and you dropped cake on me and the…" David silenced her walk down memory lane with a kiss.

"So Daddy, you ready to take your family home? Sleepless nights and thousands of diaper changes?" Allain asked with a twinkle in her eyes.

David kissed her again, "Bring it on."

Leichelle K began writing after trying to find stories reflective of the many interracial couples of the world that weren't over sexualized and extreme erotic. Her stories are mainly focused on interracial couples but include the universal themes of love, trust and being true to oneself.

Leichelle K lives in California.